THE CROSSBREED
CORNERED . . .

"Your gun, Charlie! Use your gun!
The thing's trying to kill me!" The man screamed
in rage and swung his club. The club
caught the half-breed on his hind haunch and
knocked him spinning through the air.

The crossbreed, cornered now, flung himself
straight into the man's leg . . .
his paws pumped pistonlike at the man's
chin, shredding the cloth and
digging deep gouges in his flesh.

"Get away from it, I can't shoot.
Get away!" The crossbreed, though he didn't
know why, realized he was again
at a disadvantage and, with a tremendous
leap, soared over the men's
heads, into the wilderness beyond . . .
on the run again, from the most
treacherous of all his enemies, Man . . .

BANTAM PATHFINDER EDITIONS

Bantam Pathfinder Editions provide the best in fiction and nonfiction in a wide variety of subject areas. They include novels oy classic and contemporary writers; vivid, accurate histories and biographies; authoritative works in the sciences; collections of short stories, plays and poetry.

Bantam Pathfinder Editions are carefully selected and approved. They are durably bound, printed on specially selected high-quality paper, and presented in a new and handsome format.

THE CROSSBREED
BY ALLAN W. ECKERT

With Illustrations by
KARL E. KARALUS

BANTAM PATHFINDER EDITIONS
TORONTO / NEW YORK / LONDON

A NATIONAL GENERAL COMPANY

*This low-priced Bantam Book
has been completely reset in a type face
designed for easy reading, and was printed
from new plates. It contains the complete
text of the original hard-cover edition.*
NOT ONE WORD HAS BEEN OMITTED.

THE CROSSBREED
*A Bantam Book / published by arrangement with
Little, Brown and Company*

PRINTING HISTORY
Little, Brown edition published February 1968
Reader's Digest Condensed Books edition published July 1968
Bantam Pathfinder edition published May 1970

*All rights reserved.
Copyright © 1968 by Allan W. Eckert.
This book may not be reproduced in whole or in part, by
mimeograph or any other means, without permission.
For information address: Little, Brown and Company,
34 Beacon Street, Boston, Massachusetts 02106.*

Published simultaneously in the United States and Canada

Bantam Books are published by Bantam Books, Inc., a National
General company. Its trade-mark, consisting of the words "Bantam
Books" and the portrayal of a bantam, is registered in the United
States Patent Office and in other countries. Marca Registrada.
Bantam Books, Inc., 666 Fifth Avenue, New York, N.Y. 10019.

PRINTED IN THE UNITED STATES OF AMERICA

To my good friend

HOMER S. RHODE

the greatest outdoorsman I've ever known, and with whom I have spent some of the happiest and most memorable times in my life, this book is dedicated with warmest affection and good wishes.

THE CROSSBREED

PROLOGUE

While a substantial number of the houses at the edge of this Wisconsin town were shabby, not one was quite so disreputable as the squalid, broken-porched, unpainted frame house close to the river. Its siding boards were warped and sprung, its few remaining screens askew and torn, its dirty brick chimney badly cracked and ready to collapse. Fortunately, the interior was not visible, for it was every bit as neglected.

The small front yard of this house was not only barren of grass, it was also the last resting-place of a dilapidated pickup truck, the hulk of an auto of indeterminate age and make, plus a motley collection of tin cans, washtubs, soggy cardboard and other long-accumulated trash. Except for the sickly potted geranium badly in need of water which rested on a kitchen window ledge and several sets of rather dingy long johns on a much knotted clothesline, the house might have been thought abandoned. Yet, a man lived here, and a woman, their own physical appearance little better than that of their house.

The cat that lived with them came or went at will through a bucket-sized hole in a pantry window with no screen, but she had no love for either of these humans.

Because the slovenly woman fed her on a relatively regular basis, the cat tolerated her, but no more than that. On the other hand, she feared and hated the man, who always smelled of alcohol, and she studiously avoided him at every opportunity. On more than one occasion his foot had lashed out in a vicious kick at her, and only her alertness and agility, coupled with his usual state of drunkenness, had enabled her thus far to avoid a possibly lethal blow.

Over these past weeks she moved about with extreme caution. It was close to noon when she approached the house and, as was her custom, she paused and listened before leaping lightly up to the broad sill of the pantry's broken window. Here she hesitated and listened again, and though she heard nothing to cause concern, a sudden alarm flooded her and she dropped silently to the floor and padded quickly through pantry and kitchen toward the large empty woodbox on the sagging screened veranda, where her litter of kittens was hidden.

Although this big gray cat was only a few months over four years old, this was her sixth litter and by far her largest—eleven kittens. It taxed her hunting abilities to the utmost to find food enough so that her body could produce milk in the quantity needed to satisfy these constantly hungry young ones.

As she soundlessly jumped down the single step from the kitchen to the veranda, she momentarily froze in place. Leaning over the woodbox, an old gunny sack in one hand and with his other already picking up a kitten to thrust it inside, was the man. A veritable reek of hostility emanated from him, and now even the kittens, whose pale watery-blue eyes had opened only two days ago, had begun to sense this and they raised their voices in a faint, frightened mewing.

Galvanized into instant action by the sound, the mother cat raced across the veranda and literally ran up the man's leg and backside. Her claws dug deeply through shirt and flesh and she sank her sharp teeth into his shoulder so viciously that he howled and cursed with the pain of it. He dropped bag and kitten and, using both hands, tore her away from him by brute force and flung her heavily against the wall, stunning her. She fell to the floor, and while she was still dazed, he snatched her up and plunged her into the sack, held the bulk of her form against the floor with his foot lest she recover and attempt to attack him again. In quick succession he dropped the squirming kittens into the sack after her and hastily tied the neck of the sack closed with a length of clothesline rope. With the knot secure, he slung the sack over his shoulder, wincing at the pain where the mother cat had bitten him.

The jostling, as he carried them outside, brought the female back to her senses, and though trembling with fear, she attempted to soothe her offspring with a low sound and a few licks of her tongue. After a moment she unsheathed her claws and began tearing at the bottom of the sack. She was unable to accomplish much, for the fibers stuck to her claws and she could not obtain the necessary leverage to shred them.

Then she located a fold in the sacking and met with a little more success when she attacked this portion with her teeth. In a surprisingly short time she had made a hole nearly as large as her own head. Given a few more minutes she would undoubtedly have made it large enough to escape through, but then the bag was abruptly plopped to the ground directly upon this opening. Though this made the hole more difficult to get at, nevertheless she continued to rip and chew, all the while emitting a low, fearsome growling from deep in her throat. Once again her kittens were mewing and crying in terror, unable to comprehend what was occurring.

Since the hole was on the bottom side of the sack, the man did not detect it. He scrambled awkwardly down a steep bank beside a concrete bridge crossing the Chippewa River. Here he found a large flat rock weighing fifteen pounds or more, which he laboriously carried back up to the roadway with him. Taking the long trailing end of the clothesline cord securing the neck of *the gunny sack, he knotted it tightly around this rock.*

Grunting under the increased weight, the man carried his load to the center of the bridge. He balanced it for a moment on the wide railing and then shoved it off. The weighted sack struck the water thirty feet below with a great splash, and instantly the rock pulled it to the bottom.

The unexpected shock of the cold water suddenly engulfing them was terrifying to the cat and her kittens and within the sack there was a fantastic tangle of legs and claws as each struggled frantically in his own way to get free. The large female suddenly found her head and one front leg projecting outside the bag through the hole she had made and, though she was weakening and her vision rapidly failing, she ripped at the material in a frenzy.

An interstecting seam tore a little, stopped, then tore some more, and suddenly she was free of it, being tumbled rapidly away from the bag by the swift current, at the same time gradually rising toward the surface. She broke into the air with a great wheezing gasp and then choked and coughed for some seconds before she could relieve her burning lungs with a deep inhalation.

At first it was all she could manage to remain afloat and breathe, allowing the current to sweep her along, but at last she struck out rather feebly for the nearest shore. And when, after a long while, she wearily pulled herself up onto the dry, sun-warmed gravel lining the bank of the stream, she was very weak and very sore.

She was at this point more than an eighth of a mile downstream from the bridge. Of her kittens there was no sign and she seemed to realize she would never again see them. She dragged herself even farther from the water and eventually into a small depression close against an emergent root of a large oak tree. She was too exhausted even to lick herself and hardly had she stopped moving than she had fallen into a deep sleep.

Hours later, with the sun plummeting toward the treetops rimming a hill to the west, she awoke and raised herself stiffly to all fours. For a long while she stared back upstream toward the bridge and a low, eerie sound rose in her throat.

Then she turned away and slowly entered the woods.

I

She was an unusually large gray cat.

Crouched on the ground, as she was now in this fringe area of the dense woodland at dusk, she was almost invisible, so well did her gray striping camouflage her. Except for the occasional little grating noises, caused when her gnawing teeth encountered a bone, she made no sound.

At a first, cursory glance, she appeared to be simply a cat; quite a large one, to be sure, but just an ordinary domestic cat and nothing more. On closer inspection, however, certain odd characteristics became evident which belied this initial appraisal. The very posture of her body as she crouched here, her uncommon vigilance and the penetrating and rather frightening glare of her eyes conveyed the impression that she was truly a wild creature.

She was, in fact, both.

This was a feral cat, once a domesticated animal, but now reverted, divorced from man and as thoroughly wild as any creature to be found in this west-central Wisconsin countryside. Perhaps even wilder, for more than the other wild animals of this area, she knew, feared and hated the greatest menace of all—man.

Even though she was feeding rather slowly and occasionally pausing to rest, she never really relaxed. In this deepening dusk the elliptical pupils of her eyes expanded until they became nearly round and threatened to engulf the dark greenish-yellow fields of her irises. These were incredibly keen eyes which probed her surroundings ceaselessly and with great care. Now and again one or the other of her ears would twitch and swivel slightly in order to better locate and identify some faint sound that reached her. Less frequently her chin would suddenly lift and thrust the questing nose high into the air to identify some vague scent.

Little remained of the large cottontail rabbit on the ground before her. An hour previously she had caught scent of the animal, stalked it with superb skill and pounced upon it where it crouched even before it realized the danger. A savage bite at the base of the neck had broken the rabbit's spine, and it died soundlessly. At once she had begun eating.

Now she had more than taken her fill of it and, under normal circumstances, would have gone on her way; but this was a very special time for her and she lingered, resting longer between bites, but continuing to gorge herself. It was the last she would eat for several days, and she was reluctant to leave any part of the meat behind her.

Full darkness had fallen by the time she finished eating. With meticulous care she cleansed her front paws and dense breast fur with rapid flickings of her small tongue. Then, moistening the pads of her front feet, she also scrubbed her bloodstained cheeks and muzzle and, finally, her short ears which were more rounded than tapered.

Satisfied at last, she stood and, without even another glance at the scattering of bones and fur on the ground around her, she moved out of the edge of this woodland and into an expansive prairie, heading toward a distant creek bank. She walked purposefully, but quite slowly and rather ponderously. Her belly was greatly distended and hung so very low that it practically brushed the ground as she walked. It was enlarged considerably beyond the limits any meal of rabbit could have caused, however much she might have gorged herself.

She was in the final stages of her pregnancy. Four times during her passage across this broad field she stopped as her body hunched convulsively and a faint whining cry, inaudible more than a few feet away, escaped her. These were the first signs of labor, and though as yet they were only preliminaries, time was running out. Before many more hours were to pass, she would give birth to a litter of young. Even these unborn kittens seemed aware of their impending birth, for when she stopped walking she could feel within her the strong movements of their bodies and limbs.

This was the first time since well over a year ago that she would bear young; the first since that fearful time when, after she had borne her largest litter, all eleven of them had been deliberately drowned and she very nearly with them. This would be her first litter since she had become a feral cat, since she had cut herself off irrevocably from any association with mankind and had come to depend exclusively upon her own cunning and hunting ability for survival.

Not only had she survived admirably, but she had actually thrived on this new mode of life. Her coat was darker, sleeker, glossier and much warmer than ever before, and her large body had filled out with powerful, well-proportioned muscles. She could lope along for hours at a surprisingly rapid pace now, if need be, and few indeed were the dogs who would have dared attack her by themselves. No domestic cat in this whole countryside could have stood up against her in combat. She was fierce and cunning and very wild.

Even though the offspring born of this pregnancy would not be her first, beyond any doubt they would be her most unusual, just as her mating had been, when these unborn kittens were conceived. That mating had taken place fifty-nine days ago on an unseasonably warm night in late February when the moon had been nearly as full and bright as it was now, hanging low over the trees behind her.

She had gone into heat two nights previous to that. During those intervening forty-eight hours a wide variety of tomcats from surrounding farms and outlying homes had followed the far-carrying scent of her heat-musk until they found her. But not one of them had been as large as she, and not only her size, but the overpowering fierceness and wildness of her had acted as a damper upon their enthusiasm and desire.

A few had attempted, recklessly as it turned out, to subdue her, and though she did not fight them with even near the strength and skill she could muster if necessary, nevertheless their courage faltered before her onslaught. Suddenly self-protection began to dominate even their strong sexual drive. Either they fled at top speed or else simply gave up and rolled over on their backs, signaling their surrender by exposing the vulnerable underbelly. Upon such individuals she turned her back and stalked away, and none among them had had the courage to follow.

Then, on that warm night two months ago, had come one who was different. This time it was she who felt the undercurrent of fear when the male appeared, for he was no ordinary tomcat. Although in coloration they were not too much unalike—he was spotted rather than striped and the gray of his coat had a reddish-brown cast to it—he was easily twice her size, stockily built, with dense tufts of fur on his cheeks. His ears were sharply erect, shaped not much differently from her own, except that at the very top of each was a narrow tuft of ebony hair which gave the ears a decidedly peaked appearance. In addition to being considerably longer in the body, he was much taller than she, his legs longer. His tail was extremely short, less than six inches long and blunt rather than tapered.

He was a bobcat.

This was by no means the first time that he had ever been attracted by the heat-musk of a common cat, whether domestic or feral, but it was the first time that such a cat had held her ground at his stiff-legged, rather menacing approach. Always before they had gone yowling away at top speed, and though invariably he had pursued, it was without great determination and he had soon given up the chase.

This female merely crouched low, her feet closely grouped beneath her and her muscles bunched to spring—not for flight, but undeniably for attack. A deep and far-carrying warning growl erupted from her and her long tail lashed back and forth with irregular, spasmodic jerks.

The bobcat flattened his ears against his head and then he, too, crouched and snarled softly. He moved slowly toward her in a peculiarly sinuous manner until they were only four feet apart. Still she held her ground, her own ears compressed and her eyes seeming to become almost orange in the bright moonlight. The closer he came, the louder and more threatening grew her growling. Now, as if puzzled, the bobcat stopped and for a long interval merely stared at her.

Abruptly there was a subtle change in his attitude. His growling did not cease but instead took on a new timbre—an anticipatory tone—and unconsciously he licked his lips and his short tail jerked erratically back and forth in growing excitement.

He began to circle her in a curious yet oddly graceful side-stepping movement, but she constantly shifted her own position to keep pace with him and continued to face him directly. Three complete turns were made by both of them in this manner, during which time their growls and snarlings became less muted and the surrounding woods rang with them.

Again the bobcat stopped and stared appraisingly at her. Incredibly, he seemed to lose interest. He stood upright and actually yawned and then made as if to move away. It was only a ruse, and the feral cat seemed as aware of it as the bobcat himself.

When, with hardly the preliminary swelling of a muscle to betray the movement, he launched himself at her, she was ready. In that same fractional instant she sprang to meet him. They slammed together jarringly, fell and rolled over in a ball of frenzied activity, biting, snarling, clawing and both of them screeching as loudly and frighteningly as a woman in pain or great terror.

Bits of fur tore loose and shot into the air where they wafted gently to the ground. And then, as suddenly as they had come together, the combatants drew apart and resumed their crouched positions facing each other. The snarls and screeches and caterwaulings died away to low growls and whinings.

For a little while the bobcat seemed perplexed, taken aback at the unexpected strength of this female cat, at her ferocious nature and her more than expert defense of herself. He had hardly been able to nip her and his slightly unsheathed claws had not drawn blood. Yet he himself felt the continuing pain of shallow bites received from her on his upper foreleg and flank, and his belly skin was afire from the series of scratches her own partially unsheathed claws had gouged in him.

There were certain instinctive rules to be followed in an encounter like this. The cruel hooked claws were never fully unsheathed; only an eighth of an inch at most was exposed—enough to rake through fur and skin leaving behind shallow ruts which indicated that had the opponent been serious and the claws fully unsheathed, the wounds would have been enough to disembowel rather than merely scratch. The same was true of biting; though their teeth gripped with savagery and accuracy, yet they were allowed to puncture only a little—enough to let the opponent realize what could have happened. That such instinctive rules could be so meticulously followed in the furious fur-flying melee of such an encounter was little short of miraculous.

Both animals licked their lips and once again the circling began. This time, however, scarcely one-half turn had been made when again the bobcat launched himself at the female and they clinched in a yowling, screaming ball, rolling back and forth in the little clearing.

Once again they broke apart, both of them panting a little now. This time, though a few new wounds had been inflicted upon the bobcat, the female had not come away unscathed. At least a dozen burning scratches now ran the length of her own underside, and in a half-dozen places on her throat, back, flanks and legs she had been bitten sharply.

This latest respite did not last very long. In less than half a minute after breaking apart, the feral cat bounded off to one side and raced away at top speed, the bobcat not far behind and rapidly closing the gap. With his longer legs better equipping him for speed, he overtook her before she anticipated it and bowled her over, raking her sides and haunches with his hind claws and himself getting nipped on the side of the throat in exchange.

Immediately they separated again and another chase was begun, this one circular, around a towering pine tree. Here her shorter legs were an advantage, and she not only kept ahead of him, but even gained to such an extent that for a brief while it appeared to be she who was chasing him. As if realizing that the male could not catch her as she circled like this, the feral cat abruptly veered off and began a complicated series of maneuvers: dodging around rocks, racing up into trees where she leaped from branch to branch and then back to the ground, running through hollow logs and leading her suitor on an exhausting chase. When at last he overtook her again, it was because she let him do so. Quite suddenly they were no longer fighting but running side by side, content in one another's company.

They stopped in a little copse carpeted with thick moss. A small melodious brook splashed along its stony course nearby. She rubbed her head against him and purred, and a heavier rumbling answered from him. The climax of this encounter was upon them and the mating was begun. Again the woodland echoed with their cries, but they were cries neither of anger nor of fear.

For three full days the pair was inseparable, but then a fundamental difference in their natures emerged. At each of her previous matings, the female cat and the tom who had impregnated her had quickly parted. As is the way with domestic cats, there is no lasting devotion between mates and the tom has no paternal interest in the kittens he sires. With bobcats, close bonds of affection usually develop between mates, and while they may not stay together inseparably thereafter, the male remains interested in his family. He helps to catch food for them and to train the kittens. Very frequently he stays close at hand until the young go off on their own; even then he tends to continue frequenting the female's vicinity. It is not unusual, when she goes into heat again, for them to mate and begin another family.

So now, while it was obviously the bobcat's intention to stay close, the female feral cat made it equally clear that his presence was unwelcome. For the most part she ignored him, except on those occasions when he came too close. Then she would clash with him in fierce combat, her claws and teeth fully bared and not restrained as they had been during the courtship and mating. He was always on the defensive, protecting himself against her, but not actively attempting to injure her through his own biting or clawing.

Often he stood a short distance away and stared at her with something akin to bewilderment. Not unexpectedly, his ardor diminished daily and his absences became more frequent and of longer duration. Once in a while he would approach her with a gift of some sort—a fat meadow mouse or snowshoe rabbit or young woodchuck—but she would merely turn her back and walk away, and so he stopped bringing them.

Just two weeks ago was the last time she had seen him. They had met by accident in the woods, each of them following up a fresh rabbit spoor. When she saw him, her back hunched and her hackles rose; the warning to him was implicit in her hissing growl. The bobcat had merely stood there for a long while looking at her. Then, in consummate insult to her, he defecated on the trail she had been following and ambled jauntily off.

Tonight, with the birth of her kittens close at hand, she carefully picked her way through the prairie toward the large hollow log beside the creek bank where she had prepared her nest. It was a bell-shaped hollow, just large enough to permit her entrance at the opening, then widening into a long roomy chamber on the inside, its base warmly coated with crinkly dry leaves and little bits of punky wood chips.

As always, she approached the log deviously, her senses keenly alert. She first headed directly to the creek at a point a hundred yards or more below the den. At the edge of the water she stood quietly and looked about her carefully, identifying every scent, sound and movement. A few crickets were chirping lazily, and once a bat swept by near her head, its leathery wings causing a muted fluttering sound. From a great distance came the baying of a hound and from the little grove of trees downstream came the low querulous cry of a screech owl.

Satisfied that there was nothing to fear, she stepped daintily—and a bit distastefully—into the shallows, where the water was just over the tops of her paws, and followed close to the shoreline until she was a dozen feet from the log. Sixty feet away, on the higher bank across the creek from her log, a tremendous granite boulder jutted from the earth. It was roughly round, about seven feet high and perhaps eight or ten feet in diameter. It seemed likely that as much or more of the great rock was below ground level as above.

She gave the boulder only a moment's glance and then, with a sudden bound, she sprang out of the water toward the log, cutting the gap in half. Another jump took her to the opening. She squirmed inside with difficulty, and it was obvious that had she been even a little more distended, she would not have been able to get in at all.

The instant she disappeared from sight, there was a

movement near the granite boulder. The animal who had been crouching there at its base, hidden by deep grasses, now stood erect and for several minutes gazed quietly at the log. A deep, soft rumble sounded in his throat—a strangely wistful sort of noise—and then he turned and loped smoothly off, his tufted ears high and his blunt little bobtail held at a jaunty angle.

II

In the absolute darkness, his first sensation was one of warmth; a pervading, constant, all-encompassing warmth in which the organism that was himself seemed suspended. There was a timelessness filled only with that warmth and a continuous growth as cells divided and redivided and redivided again.

There was a formlessness about the organism which gradually changed into indeterminate shapes and these shapes themselves grew and became more sharply delineated and detailed. There was movement of a sort, not his own, but rather an alien, outside movement, a jarring or rhythmic bumping at intervals which was more sensed than felt.

Then there was movement, too, of a different sort, a self-motivated movement: the tentative first flexing of a muscle here and the stretching of another there, the swiveling of his tiny head on its axis and the arching of his little spine. Minute bones, yet elastic, became harder, stronger, and new blood began developing in the marrow of those bones to supplement that from an outer source. It entered the miniature circulatory system and, as a diminutive heart suddenly began to pulse with a regular strong cadence, helped to augment the body's ever-growing need for oxygen, which was brought to him arterially from outside.

A new dimension came with the sense of touch, for one of his outstretched limbs touched another separate small organism which responded with its own movement; and occasionally after that there would come the sensation of a limb not his own nudging him and he would squirm in response.

Increasingly, the previously roomy darkness was no longer expansive, and no longer was there that floating sensation, but rather one of pressure and not uncomfortable closeness. Every movement he made elicited a responsive movement from that which pressed against him.

The closeness soon lost its pleasantness and comfort and became cramped. He was thumped frequently, solidly, and when this occurred, he thrust out his own legs in reaction and always they pushed against a flexible firmness in every direction. The need to stretch, to move freely, became dominant and then, for the first time, there came pain—a great compressive spasm which gripped and hurt him, relaxed, then came again and repeated itself at closer intervals, until existence became no more than peaks and valleys of pain and not-pain.

Finally there came a numbing pressure which did not abate, and he separated from the organisms around him and in the perpetual darkness was thrust along in one direction. Momentarily the surging movement stopped, but then it came back with irresistible force, shoving him now in a great burst of power against a barrier so strong that he was being crushed.

With explosive suddenness there came a great expulsive movement and he was free for the first time of the pressure. A thin bluish membrane still enshrouded him, and through it—sensed rather than actually seen—came an awareness of light; and through it as well came a penetrating cold and he shivered and kicked.

A soft and warm, yet rasping organ gently lapped

away the membranous material, first from his limbs and
body, and then from his head. For the first time in his
brief existence, fresh air entered his nostrils and inflated
his little lungs. He exhaled that breath and, with it, a
barely audible mewing sound, little more than a
squeak.

The crossbreed was born.

He was the first of the crossbred kittens born of the
feral cat and, as soon became apparent, the largest. He
was also the only male in a litter of five and, of that
quintet, the most obviously different in appearance.

Two of the female kittens, born shortly after him,
bore the general markings of their bobcat sire. This was
evident when, after they had been licked clean by their
dam, their fur became dry and warm and fluffy. These
markings were not so pronounced, of course, on their
short hair, but there was indication of pattern enough
to show that, in maturity, they would be spotted rather
than striped and resemble him in markings, if not in
color. One of the remaining two females was a deep,
sooty gray with darker charcoal stripes intermingled
with scattered spottings. The final female kitten appeared in every respect to be a normal gray-striped
domestic kitten. Except for the spot markings on the
first two, none of these four bore any substantial resemblance to the bobcat.

The male crossbreed, however, was larger by at least
a third than any of his litter mates, with decidedly
longer legs and larger feet than they possessed. His
markings were virtually identical to the stripes worn by
his mother, but the basic undercolor of the fur leaned
more to the grayish buff-red of his sire, and already it
was evident that he would have the full-tufted cheeks
and small pointed ear tufts of the bobcat.

One other characteristic of appearance instantly and
incontrovertibly set him apart from the other four.
Each of the females had the normally short, tapered
tail of the house kitten—a tail which would become
long and supple as they matured—but the tail of this

little male crossbreed was a duplicate in miniature of his sire's: a true bobtail.

All five of the kittens were born within a span of twenty minutes, and for the next half hour—following ejection of the placental mass, which she promptly devoured—the large feral cat licked them clean and they dried rapidly. Though they were blind and their eyes would remain sealed for perhaps another nine or ten days, instinctively now they crept toward the warmth of their mother's underside.

The large male kitten got there first and was also first to find and greedily take into his mouth one of the nipples. He tugged and sucked, and in a moment there came a flood of warm, satisfying milk. He drank until his stomach bulged to such an extent that it appeared he had swallowed a tennis ball. Without relinquishing his grip, the male kitten fell asleep. This little sequence more or less set the pattern of existence for all of them over the next three days.

During that time the large female licked and cleaned and nuzzled them tenderly and frequently, leaving the den only twice. Once, near the end of the second day after their birth, she slipped out of the log's opening—which now was not so tight for her passage—and, after a cautious look all around, padded to the creek where she drank very deeply. Within two minutes she was back inside the log.

Her passage had not gone unobserved. Once again the bobcat arose from his watching post beside the granite boulder, and this time when he set off, after she had disappeared back inside the log, it was with a determined trotting gait and he did not look back.

In the forenoon of the third day, with the rabbit she had eaten long since digested, a great hunger blossomed in the feral cat. By sunset she was so hungry she was trembling. Disengaging herself from the nursing kittens, who mewed plaintively, she stood, and moved to the entrance where she peered out cautiously.

Although while inside with her offspring she had remained alert for any suspicious sound and had heard nothing, a few feet away from the entrance lay the carcass of a large snowshoe rabbit. Instantly wary, she merely looked at it for a long while, at the same time listening intently for any suspicious sound and sniffing the air for possible scent of danger.

At length she left the log and circled the dead animal. It was quite stiff and had undoubtedly been lying there since early morning, perhaps since before daybreak. Gingerly she came closer to the rabbit. When she caught the faint scent of her bobcat mate on the rabbit's fur, she relaxed. She straightened and looked around in all directions. Except for a loose formation of crows flying low on the evening horizon, there seemed to be nothing moving. After a moment she dipped her head, picked up the rabbit by its head and half dragged, half carried it to the hollow log.

She dropped the animal there and disappeared into the opening, only to reappear an instant later and lean out to pick up the carcass in her teeth and tug it inside. Because its legs were stiff with rigor mortis, she experienced some difficulty in the process, but at last she managed to yank it through and drag it nearly to the nest area.

Without hesitation she attacked it, first tearing open the abdomen and eating the vital organs, and then settling down to a solid feast of the nourishing meat. She waited until she had fully satisfied her own hunger before she gave in to the plaintive mewing of the kittens, who had become increasingly restive and were now crawling all over one another in their pathetic, blind search for her.

While the kittens nursed, she cleaned herself and then licked each of them thoroughly. It was during this close cleansing of them that a curious thing occurred. The stimulation of her tongue lapping their soft bellies caused each of the kittens, in turn, to eliminate whatever wastes had been stored up in its body. As these wastes appeared, the feral cat merely lapped them up as well, thereby preventing the nest area from quickly becoming a foul mess. This was a natural process she would continue for many days, at least until their eyes opened and they began to venture outside regularly.

The bobcat seemed to be aware of exactly how much food his mate would need, for while she ate regularly from the carcass of the rabbit during the night, through the fourth day and the night which followed, no more offerings were left. By the fifth morning, however, all that remained of the rabbit was bits of fur and bone which were shoved to one side, but when she left the hollow just before sunup to drink, she found another rabbit—a cottontail this time—in the same place where the snowshoe rabbit had been deposited.

Although again she had heard no sound outside, the carcass was still warm. Obviously, the rodent had been dead for no more than fifteen or twenty minutes. Quickly she looked all around again, but her mate was not visible, and at last she walked to the creek and drank deeply.

She ran downstream a dozen yards or so where she pawed a small hole in the sand, relieved herself in it, covered the droppings and then returned to the log. She picked up the flaccid rabbit carcass and carried it into the den.

A few minutes later she reappeared, leaped to the top of the log den and sat there without movement for many minutes. Several hundred yards away in the edge of the woods, a doe flicked her tail and the cat saw her instantly. Far out in the meadow a woodchuck briefly raised his head above the new emerald grasses, and she saw him, too. Newly arrived from the south, a killdeer ran for several feet along the gravel of the creekbed, fifty yards or so upstream, and she saw it. But of the bobcat she saw no sign.

As a matter of fact, she never saw him again.

III

Their eyes had opened on the ninth day—pale, light blue eyes which did not begin to assume their true lifetime coloration until now, in their sixth week. It appeared that three of the little females would have eyes the color of their mother's; a deep yellow-green. The fourth female's were very decidedly green without any trace of yellow.

It was not so easy, however, to determine the color of eyes the little male crossbreed would have. At various times and under different light conditions they seemed to change; often a yellowish-orange, sometimes faintly greenish, but always with a distinct gray cast to them.

By this sixth week the kittens were becoming well developed physically and, while they still had the appearance of kittens, they could now walk and run without getting all tangled up in their own legs and sprawling, as they had done previously. They were insatiably curious and already were learning from their mother the rudiments of hunting and self-defense which must stand them in good stead for the rest of their lives. As the result of two separate occurrences, they also had learned from her a pronounced fear of humans.

The first incident itself was nothing spectacular, but the reaction of the large gray feral cat was little short of startling. The kittens were still less than a month old on that occasion, when a lone, walking man had suddenly come into view some distance away on the prairie. Extremely interested in this strange-looking, two-legged creature, the little male crossbreed—who was first to see him—had begun a clumsy run in that direction to get a better look.

He didn't get far.

With almost brutal unexpectedness his mother overtook him and literally pounced upon him, nailing him to the ground beneath her and at the same time giving vent to a strange, hissing growl which made the kitten's own startled outcry die aborning. The four little females had immediately flattened themselves against the ground at their mother's warning, and their fright was a direct reflection of their mother's own deep fear. She shivered as if from severe cold and her eyes had become wide and wild. Her initial cry had degenerated into a continuous, whining snarl, low and filled with malevolence and near panic.

Actually, the man never came very close to them and neither saw the cat family nor even suspected its presence. Nevertheless, none of the animals moved from their flattened positions until he had disappeared into the distant woods. Only then, with a sort of choppy, grunting sound, the feral cat led them in a low run back to the den log fifty yards away, and there they remained hidden for the rest of the day.

If the young ones were unable to understand her seemingly unreasonable fear at that time, the incident which had occurred last week left them with no doubt as to why this two-legged being should be so feared and avoided.

Although their bobcat father had been in the vicinity of the den a good bit, as evidenced by the continued food offerings left behind, they had never seen him until this time. His appearance then left an indelible impression in their minds and a fear as permanent and pronounced as their mother's.

Shortly after dawn, when the feral cat had been gone from the den for more than an hour on a solitary hunting expedition, a curious, distant sound caught the kittens' attention. They should have remained well hidden in the deepest recesses of the hollow log den, but they could not resist a peek at what was creating the peculiar sound. One by one, five little heads poked from the entrance, and in this dim morning light they finally saw their sire.

The bobcat was angling toward the creekbed from the closest point of woods and he seemed to be having an uncommonly difficult time. While it was apparent that he would reach the waterway some distance upstream from them—perhaps fifty feet or more above the big boulder and on that same side of the creek— they could see him clearly. His movements were bewildering to watch: he would lunge forward for a dozen feet or more through the old prairie grass and then abruptly draw back a little and sink down, exhausted, only to leap up again in a moment and repeat the process. Not until he reached the edge of the high bank, however, were the kittens able to see what was wrong. He poised for a moment there, gasping loudly enough for them to hear, and then attempted to climb down the eight feet or so into the stony creekbed.

Clinging to the bobcat's right rear foot was a heavy steel trap with a long chain stretched out behind it. To this chain was wired a drag—a piece of branch, six inches in diameter, forked and about five feet long— and it was this object that had been so impeding his progress.

For a moment, at this point, the drag held him back, caught by the heavy tangled grasses, but then it jerked free and tumbled over the creek bank onto the stones after him. Regaining his balance, the bobcat thrust his muzzle down and lapped the cold water thirstily. When he had finished, he once more began his flight, hidden from above by the bank and heading upstream, away from the den log where the wide-eyed kittens watched in fearful fascination. But the bobcat had gone no more than a dozen feet when the drag became wedged tightly between some rocks. No amount of pulling or jerking on his part could free it.

At last, breathing heavily from his efforts, he lay down on the gravel bank and began to lick and nuzzle his foot and bite in frustration at the powerful steel jaws holding it. Already the trapped foot was swollen to nearly twice its normal size. The pain of it must have been terrible, but the bobcat made no outcry.

The sun was just above the horizon when the humans came, and from the moment they left the woods and entered the prairie it was obvious they were following the bobcat's trail. Nor was it a difficult trail to follow, since the drag had gouged the ground and torn the grasses and brush as it was pulled along.

They were smaller humans than the one the kittens had seen a dozen days ago at a distance, but their demeanor was much much more frightening. One of them carried a heavy stick and the other a small-caliber rifle, though the kittens could not comprehend at this time what it was.

The bobcat, hidden from view of the trackers by the high bank, heard the humans coming and then lunged frantically to pull his foot free of the trap. He jerked too hard, and the effort snapped the bone of his leg at the point where the jaws of the trap gripped it. By then the youths had reached the creek bank and, hooting with glee at their catch, were scrambling down to the stream bed, keeping a respectful distance from the large animal.

Half sitting on his haunches with the high bank at his back, the bobcat snarled menacingly and then backed off a little. Apparently uncertain how next to proceed, the pair hurriedly discussed the matter. The youth with the rifle was evidently in favor of shooting their quarry from a safe distance and once even began

raising the gun, but his companion stopped him. A bullet hole would damage the hide, and he wanted to tan it in order to make a small trophy rug.

They conversed some more, and then the one with the rifle stepped back and held it at ready. The other, brandishing his club, moved forward gingerly until just out of range of the animal and then began poking the stick at him. Time after time the bobcat lunged, swatted at the stick and attempted to reach his tormentor, but he could not. At last he fell exhausted and lay on his stomach glaring and snarling at the youth with the club.

Suddenly the boy brought the stick down hard upon the bobcat's head, partially stunning him. The animal, knocked onto his side, struggled to control his legs and get them under him, but exhaustion and pain and the heavy blow had taken their toll. The next crushing strike caught him at the base of his neck and broke his spine.

He fell over in a strained position, his legs stiff and an involuntary shuddering causing his whole body to tremble. In a moment the shaking stopped as his body relaxed permanently in death. The youth poked the stick fearfully at the carcass several times until certain the bobcat was really dead and not just unconscious. Then both boys advanced to inspect their prize.

They rubbed their hands through the dense fur, touched the teeth and ears and looked at the fearsome claws. The lad who had killed him then released the foot from its imprisonment, snipped the wire holding the trap to its drag and dropped the device into a large deep pocket of his coat. With that same piece of wire he bound all four feet tightly together and then thrust his stick from front to back between the legs. Each of the boys then took up an end of the stick and set off with the bobcat hanging pendulously between them.

With difficulty they regained the top of the bank, dropping the bobcat twice in the process. Five minutes later they had disappeared in the direction whence they had come. Now mewing with fear, the kittens scrambled back deep into their haven. There, in the dimly lighted interior, they huddled together in a trembling cluster, still wailing and very much alone.

It was more than an hour later when their mother returned, carrying with her a plump fox squirrel she had caught. The kittens were still frightened and though she was alarmed, she could not understand what had caused their fear. She licked them reassuringly until their fears were dissolved.

Although these kittens were still nursing from the feral cat and would continue to do so for yet another fortnight, nevertheless they were showing increasing interest in more solid foods. When their mother began eating the squirrel, they joined her. Comical little tugs-of-war, replete with ferocious growls, resulted as two or more of them vied for the same piece of meat. After they were filled, bits of fur and bones suddenly became prey for them. Instinctively they would sink low, eyes locked on their stationary target and creep slowly and stealthily toward it in a remarkably able mimicry of their own mother's hunting method.

Occasionally, too, they stalked one another, pouncing upon an unsuspecting litter mate and tumbling over and over in furious—and often ludicrous—battle. Their mother's tail was also an interesting object to stalk and attack, but they quickly learned not to bite it too hard—her lightning-quick forepaw could deal a heavy blow.

Another highly favored pastime was peeping at the outside world from a unique and unusually handy observation post. Far back inside the den where the cavity of the log narrowed sharply, there was a hole which went upward straight through the center of a hollow, broken-off limb rising like a periscope from the top of the log for a distance of about fifteen inches. It was too small a hollow for the adult cat to enter, but with a little maneuvering, one of the kittens—even the larger male crossbreed—could squirm upward until his head projected from the opening in the stub.

From this point the surroundings of the den could be viewed with perfect immunity, for if danger in any form threatened, the kitten need only draw his head in, as if he were a gopher, and then scramble backwards down the hole into the den proper. Even more than the others, the little male crossbreed seemed to enjoy perching here and often he peered from it for hours at a stretch.

Except for the two separate appearances of their human enemies, it was a happy time for the kittens. They grew stronger and more sure of themselves, and at the end of the sixth week after their birth, began in earnest their hunting lessons from the feral cat. They ventured farther and farther from the den area, often frozen in a crouched cluster as they watched their mother stalk and kill her prey.

This instruction had begun with the stalking of meadow mice, but the kittens soon graduated to larger creatures—mainly ground squirrels, rabbits and young woodchucks—and while none of them had yet successfully stalked and caught any manner of prey by themselves, they could hardly have had a better instructor than their mother. She was a consummate hunter.

One heavily overcast morning she and the kittens—the male crossbreed, as always, the closest on her heels —set out up the creek past the big rock. They kept on the gravel-bed area until the creek entered the deeper woods perhaps a quarter mile from their den. Here they left the waterway and were traveling silently in single file through the forest when the gray feral cat stopped and, at the same instant, flattened against the ground. At once her offspring emulated the action.

A low sound issued from their mother, and they held their places even though she slunk to one side into a screen of brush and broken branches. Losing sight of her, the kittens automatically looked ahead to see what had interested her. At first they saw nothing, so well was the animal camouflaged by its protective coloring, but then it moved a little, and five sets of keen little eyes locked on it instantly.

The prey was a large snowshoe rabbit, amazingly inconspicuous in its summer colors of drab rusty-brown sprinkled with darker guard hairs. There was a small patch of black on the top of its short, fluffy tail, and this same black was repeated on the back side of each of its ear tips. Behind the rabbit a mass of windfallen timber lay, through which a dense thicket of speckled alder scrub was pushing its way upward some twenty feet. Against this background the rodent was virtually invisible except when it moved.

At the moment the rabbit was moving very little, not really having cause to, since it was squatting in the midst of some sort of tender low vegetation growing profusely there and upon which it was busily engrossed in feeding. Even so, the rabbit was wary in the extreme, rarely keeping its head down for more than three or four seconds at a time, just long enough to nibble off another succulent piece of greenery. Then up the head would come, and the bulging eyes would peer all around, suspiciously.

The windfall of shattered timber was in a small basinlike swale of the forest floor and therefore somewhat lower than the point at which the kittens lay watching so intently. Most of the time they could see both the rabbit and their own mother. The large gray feral cat had appeared on the other side of the brush, paused there briefly as if estimating the height of the slight rise between herself and the rodent, then began a swift, soundless run in a position so incredibly crouched that it was amazing she could run that way. Her body became greatly elongated and her stomach was practically flat against the ground. As she ran in this manner, the line from the top of her head to the tip of her tail was so level that she seemed rather to flow than run.

In a very short time she had made a wide circle around the rabbit on its leeward side so that no trace of her own scent would reach and alarm the rodent. In less than a minute from the time she had left her kittens, she was peering at her intended prey from the final effective concealment of the alder-grown windfall.

Now there was no real cover to speak of between her and the snowshoe rabbit; perhaps a tall spindly weed here and a short tuft of grass there, but nothing really substantial behind which she might reasonably have been expected to conceal herself. The distance separating the two was still twenty feet or even more, far too much to be covered by a sudden headlong rush from this hiding place before the quarry took alarm and escaped with its uncanny running and dodging ability.

The feral cat's crouched gait now became one of even greater stealth as she flattened her body against the earth and virtually flowed into the open. Not for a single instant did her gaze leave the rabbit, and she moved only when its head was down for those brief seconds of nibbling. It was incredible how she took advantage of every conceivable object to break up her outline; even grasses no more than an inch or two in height helped miraculously to conceal her. Step by excruciatingly slow step, she inched forward, stretching out until at times her length seemed doubled and her slinking form was more like that of a great sinuous ferret than a cat. Her tail was straight out behind her, and just the very tip of it was twitching nervously.

Time after time it seemed that the rabbit couldn't possibly help seeing her; yet just as often, its head would dip to nibble again and the crucial gap separating them would be decreased by another inch or so. The only movement the feral cat made, besides her gradual forward progress and the faint, anticipatory jerking of her tail tip, was when a stub of grass brushed across her eyeball and caused her to blink rapidly several times.

Suddenly, they were only five feet apart. The time for stealth was past. With a tremendous bound, the cat sprang at her prey. The reflexes of the rabbit were impressive, and in that fraction of time, while the cat was in midair, it realized its peril and gave a mighty leap to one side. It was an admirable effort which came only a hairsbreadth too late.

The gray cat caught the rabbit with a paw on each side of its body, her deadly claws digging deeply into its flanks and tearing the flesh until they gripped solidly the thick thigh muscles of both hind legs. At the same time her jaws closed in a great bite over the rodent's lower back, and together they rolled over and over in a flailing, kicking tangle.

Abruptly it was all over. The spine of the rabbit snapped and the animal went limp. For several seconds longer the feral cat maintained her hold; then at last she let go and stood erect. A loud, triumphant yowling cry escaped her. At this sound the kittens came to life and tumbled excitedly onto the scene, falling all over themselves and each other in their haste to get there.

The little male crossbreed was the first on the scene by ten feet. He flung himself headlong at the rabbit and rolled over with it. His teeth were buried in the animal's throat and his hind claws tore in deadly earnest at the flaccid body. Then the other kittens arrived in group and they too pounced on the carcass, clawing and biting, as the glen resounded with their shrill mews and squeaky growls.

Before they had tired of worrying the carcass, however, the parent cat nudged them aside, picked up the bedraggled form across the middle of the back and began trotting away toward the creek bank. The kittens fell in behind her dutifully and now and then pounced upon the rabbit's dragging hind feet.

They had reached the creekbed but had not yet left the woods behind them when heavy rumblings of thunder began booming over the hills. The feral cat paused and glanced nervously in that direction for several seconds, then continued toward the den at a faster pace. A heavy rainstorm was in the making, and she was uneasy. She had always disliked getting wet, and since that time last year when she had very nearly been drowned, her aversion to water was pronounced.

For a while it was debatable which would get to the hollow log den first—the gray cat and her family or the storm. It was a close race, indeed, but they won it. Hardly had they entered the chamber, the feral cat dragging the rabbit in behind them, when it seemed that the heavens had split. A veritable torrent of rain

slashed down; its furious drumming on the hollow log was almost deafening.

Since the kittens had already been through several brief rainstorms, they were not particularly perturbed by this one. Still, when lightning cracked nearby it caused them to jump involuntarily and cower for a moment. It was, as the parent cat had known it would be, quite a bad storm, but it did not discourage the young ones from tearing into the rabbit. They ate some of it, though not really very much, and then turned to their preferred diet of milk. While her offspring suckled, the mother cat continued to feed on the rabbit. She was trembling slightly, and it was obvious that she was considerably more bothered by the storm than were her kittens.

The rain fell heavily with little abatement. A small trickle of water, which entered that periscope-like hollow stub at the rear of the den, ran along a narrow groove in the den floor, past the cat and her nursing kittens, and then trickled out the opening in a steady stream.

There was still a good bit of meat remaining when the feral cat finished eating. She pushed the carcass to one side and washed herself thoroughly. All five of her kittens, pleasantly weary from their exciting outing, had fallen sound asleep at the nipples. Except for one or two weakly murmured protests, they hardly moved when she cleaned them. That chore finished, the adult cat herself shrugged down into a more comfortable position and dropped quickly into a deep sleep.

She was no longer trembling. The drumming of the rain was, after all, a soothing sound and the inhabitants of this log den had a safe, dry, warm and quite comfortable place to wait out the storm.

At any rate, so it seemed.

IV

All day and all night the storm raged, occasionally letting up briefly, but then slashing back in a short while with renewed vigor. Certainly it was bad enough where the hollow log den of the feral cat was located, but it was considerably worse in the hilly country to the northeast.

Not until midmorning of the following day, with the rain still coming down in a more or less steady downpour, did the big female show any increase in her initial apprehension. Twice she stuck her head from the opening of the den and directed her gaze at the adjacent creek. Before the rain had begun, it was a small stream, no more than a few yards across and relatively shallow except for a few deep pools. So many rocks projected above the surface that in most places it was possible to get across easily without even getting a foot wet. But since yesterday the water had risen and spread alarmingly. A few of the previously visible rocks still showed above the surface, and around these few boulders the water swished and gurgled menacingly.

Where, before, the den log had been four or five feet above the water level and some twelve feet from the shoreline, now the roily waters were only a foot or so away and mere inches below the level of the base of the log. The feral cat's apprehension returned in force then, and by noon she had taken up a steady vigil of the stream from the entranceway of the den. When and if the water came to the base of the log, she would begin moving her offspring to higher ground, but she was loath to do so unless it became positively essential.

At last the rainfall began slackening and the creek level held steady. Within an hour the water had even withdrawn a few inches. Satisfied that her family was now in no immediate danger, she re-entered the bell-shaped chamber of the den, finished eating the remains of the snowshoe rabbit and settled down again with her kittens.

On their part, the young animals showed little concern for anything except feeding. They nursed heavily from her, submitted unprotestingly to her cleansing and promptly fell asleep again. Somewhat thirsty herself, the feral cat merely stretched out her head a little way and lapped up some of the fresh, cool water in the diminishing rivulet still dribbling past in the groove on the den floor. Though the rainstorm wasn't very pleasant, it had provided this unexpected advantage.

In spite of the fact that the downpour had considerably abated in this immediate vicinity, it was still raining very heavily some distance up the creek. There were in this area, within the span of a mile, two beaver dams. The lower one was the larger of these, and though much smaller than the biggest dams in the area, it was still quite an extensive and sturdy affair. From one end to the other it was over five hundred feet long, and at no point was it less than nine feet high. Generation after generation of beavers had continued building what only a pair had begun many years ago. Over the years nearly two hundred tons of material had been put into its construction by those energetic rodents, and by this time it backed up a very significant body of water, virtually a lake.

The upper dam had a much smaller impoundment behind it and was itself less than one hundred feet in length. Though it was newer than the lower dam, it was still many years old and, like the lower one, was still being added to every year. On one end, where it attached to a high undercut bank, the hulking, branchless trunk of a once massive tree still stood. A decade before, it had been struck by lightning and snapped off jaggedly twenty-five feet above the ground. The portion that had fallen had mostly moldered away, and now this towering stump, over three feet in diameter, barkless and weathered to a gray-white, stood guarding the impoundment as if it were some sturdy lighthouse.

When the runoff of the present excessive rainfall on the hills still farther above began pouring over the lowest point of the upper dam, that point was right against this undercut bank. For a considerable while the bank held out against the strong waters rushing past, but then a large glacial rock suddenly washed loose and dropped out of the bank into the current. At once the swirling waters rushed into the cavity it left behind, and in moments, chunks of the bank began caving in from the rupture.

What followed then was inevitable. Eventually the erosion so weakened the bank that it was no longer able to support the multitonned weight of the towering stump, and it leaned precariously. Long dead roots popped with the sound of guns being fired, and then the massive trunk thundered down and struck the dam squarely with a crushing blow.

The dam split and then burst, and a great surge of water pushed through, tearing out even more of the dam and carrying the big stump along with it. The pressure of the water was tremendous and the current frightening. Though it took some distance for the trunk to pick up speed, by the time it reached the lower dam it was an irresistible juggernaut sweeping along.

Water was already going over the top of the lower dam at a considerable volume, but it was spread out over a wide expanse. More than likely, the dam would have held and suffered little real damage had it not been for the great stump. With the fantastic driving power of some heavily laden freight train, the trunk smashed into the midsection of the lower dam and virtually blew it apart. A massive wall of water—the combined contents now of both impoundments—roared through the gap, swiftly ripping away still greater chunks of the construction, until the width of the break was at least one hundred yards and still spreading.

The water crashed down the little creekbed in a wave five or six feet higher than the already swollen creek level. It was a fearsome spectacle. The water left its banks and spread out over the creek valley, but even this did little to diminish its awesome power and speed. Dozens of trees in its path were pushed down as it struck, became entangled with others and piled up in grotesque, interlocking monuments.

The feral cat heard it coming long before it arrived, for the very ground vibrated with its thunder. Again she stuck her head out nervously to investigate. The creek still seemed relatively normal here, but the roaring through the woods grew ever louder and now she could hear the loud crackings and snaps as limbs and trunks splintered and broke.

She didn't know what it was, but instinctively she knew it was deadly and that she and her kittens were in the path of it. Turning, she leaped back into the chamber. She snatched up the first kitten she encountered—the very dark, green-eyed female—and sped with her out through the opening and across the prairie just as the great wall of water, filled with branches and debris, burst from the woods and spread out toward them.

Though the mother cat was swift, even with the well-grown kitten in her mouth, the water was much faster. Thundering down on them, it smashed into the great boulder with a hideous noise and, an instant later, swept up the den log as if it were no more than the merest of twigs and threw it back into its watery maw. A small furry creature catapulted out of the open end of it in a high arc, struck the water, disappeared beneath the surface and did not rise again.

A moment more and the wave had caught up to the

fleeing, panic-stricken feral cat, smashing her with its hammer blow, wrenching the kitten from her mouth and sweeping it into oblivion. Though she was strong, she was powerless against the brutal torrent. Twice her head appeared briefly on the turbulent surface, her eyes bulging and her front feet flailing in a desperate effort to stay afloat, but she was sucked under again. This time she did not reappear.

The log, in the meanwhile, bucked and bounced in this awful maelstrom. Its upper portion had for decades been drying in the sun and was, as a result, extremely buoyant, but the bottom of it had been absorbing the moisture of the earth upon which it had lain and this portion was decidedly not buoyant.

Not able to keep up with the fantastic crest at first, the log had dropped considerably behind that great destructive wave. The swirling waters in which it floated were deep and very swift, but now they were not quite so turbulent, and the log maintained a more even keel. Because of the weight of its waterlogged bottom, only the upper eight or ten inches of its surface remained above water; the entranceway to the hollow and the entire interior of the den itself were submerged. The hollow upright branch took on the appearance of a periscope, and the log itself became the submarine body with decks barely awash.

Within the water-filled den were the drowned bodies of two kittens, and inside the hollow branch stub was the male crossbreed kitten, still alive, soaked and terrified beyond measure, wedged miraculously into the one spot where he might yet live.

His eyes were tightly closed and his head pressed firmly into his forelimbs, while his feet and legs and body ached from the desperation with which he dug in his claws and clung to the wood of this strange tubelike haven. A mournful wailing cry left him and was lost in the overwhelming gurgling of the waters. After that single outcry he remained silent.

Time after time the log struck objects beneath the water's surface. When this happened, the log would tilt sharply to one side or another, the hollow branch would plunge momentarily under the surface, then come upright again. And inside the branch the kitten would, each time, cough and gag and sputter, but not once did he relax his desperate grip against the inner side.

At one point the den log slammed with jarring impact into a massive oak tree projecting from the water, and the blow partially stunned the little crossbreed. Still, he somehow managed to maintain his tenacious hold. A short while later, the bottom of the log caught against something which snagged it firmly and held. The pressure of the water behind pushed the log deeper under the surface until only a portion of the stub itself still projected. Inside, the water level came up frighteningly all the way to the kitten's shoulders, but, despite his terror, he held on.

For many long minutes the log stayed in this new position and now the coldness of the water was numbing him. His teeth chattered uncontrollably and once again he gave voice to the miserably desolate wailing. Finally, another log, smaller than his own, came along and bumped solidly into the submerged den. The force of this blow was enough to free the den log from whatever it was that had snagged it so tightly. Once again the uppermost part of the log bobbed above the surface, and the water in the little crossbreed's tube drained away from him into the den below. He was shivering violently.

The current had become a little slower now, but because the log rode almost directly over the old creek bed, it continued to be swept along. Fully three miles below the spot where the kitten had been born, the creek emptied into the Chippewa River, and the log bobbed along easily and entered the greater current of this good-sized stream.

At this point the den log turned completely around once and then arrowed downstream, its speed once again increasing. The current was quite strong, and though the effect of the wall of water that had swept into this river—and was still coming at a good rate—was certainly apparent, it had not caused the devastation here that had taken place farther up the feeder creek.

In that first heavy wash a number of trees had gone down and quite a few others were partially uprooted and leaning with the current. The water here was considerably above the level it normally acquired when swollen by heavy rains upstream, but the banks were higher as well. Though in some low-lying areas there was extensive flooding, it was decidedly a more gradual and, therefore, a less destructive form of flooding.

In the area that the log reached after another hour of floating down the central channel of the Chippewa River, the effects of the beaver dam's bursting so high above were relatively moderate. The water level was still a good bit higher than mere rains should have made it, and the current was undoubtedly greater than ever, but actual water damage here was at a minimum.

Most of the larger trees and branches that had been washed along in that initial smashing onslaught had now lodged against other trees still standing and which projected from the water. There was still a considerable amount of smaller debris floating along—mainly twigs, short logs and little branches—and it was in the midst of this that the den log continued to float. In some ways, in fact, the material tended to keep the bigger log in the main river channel.

For the crossbreed kitten, the ride was much smoother now than it had been during those awful early minutes. Since all the debris was drifting at approximately the same speed, only rarely did anything of substantial size thump into the log. On such occasions the nudge was not strong enough to cause the upward projecting stub of branch to dip beneath the surface again.

The consistent gray of this day's sky became deeper with the encroaching twilight, and night fell with surprising abruptness; and yet the log drifted. Within the hollow stub the little crossbreed still clung—soggy, cold, weak, hungry, terrified and appearing much more dead than alive.

But alive, nonetheless.

V

All through the night the den log drifted downstream at a reasonably steady rate. Once in a while it would lodge for a short interval, but then break free when another chunk of drifting wood nudged it; and one time it was caught in an eddy where, for nearly an hour, it circled slowly until a vagrant current caught it and pulled it away.

Just as the first wan streaks of dawn were lighting the eastern sky, the den log entered the Mississippi River at the foot of that broad expanse known as Lake Pepin. The little crossbreed did not even notice. His eyes were closed, and only the infrequent opening and closing of his mouth indicated he was still alive.

The daylight came bright and clear, with the sky swept clean of clouds and no trace of haziness in the crisp atmosphere. Along the shoreline of the river a variety of birds sang and flitted about, many of them engaged in wooing mates, establishing territorial rights or seeking out nesting material. Few, if any, paid particular attention to the mostly sunken log slowly drifting by. None heard the occasional faint cry, the weak and pitiful little moaning which came from the stub of the branch sticking straight up from the log.

The crossbreed felt a pervading numbness, and it took a major effort on his part merely to raise his head. Every now and then he moved one of his legs a little in an attempt to ease his cramped position, but even this required complete concentration and was accomplished only with much difficulty. Even worse than this quasi-paralysis was the nauseous feeling which enveloped him. For over fourteen hours he had been bobbing along in his tiny haven with not an instant's cessation of movement, and he was queasy and dizzy.

The little crossbreed's prospects for survival at this time—as they had been ever since the great wave struck—were exceedingly dim. Even if, through some fortunate happenstance, he managed to get safely to shore, he would very likely starve to death, since he was not experienced enough, agile enough or even strong enough now to catch any manner of prey.

The brightness of the first rays of sunshine beginning to slant into the upper rim of his stub seemed to hearten him some, and he began a movement of sorts to the top. It was a miserably slow and painful process. Extreme physical effort was needed merely to disengage the claws of one of his front feet from its purchase in order to let it creep upward only a fraction of an inch. Then even greater concentration was required to force the claws to dig securely into the tough wood again before releasing the grip held by the other front paw. His rear quarters had been in water far more than the front, yet they reacted to his climbing much more easily.

Nevertheless, progress was inordinately slow. Even though the crossbreed's head was no more than six or seven inches from the opening to begin with, it took him an hour to reach the top and raise his head into the open air. His eyes were crusted with mucus, and he could open them only a little. The sight of all this water surrounding him, more water than ever before, once again set him to trembling in fear.

The log was now downstream from that wide portion called Lake Pepin, and though the Mississippi was a huge river at this point, it was not so vast as it would become much farther downstream when joined successively by such rivers as the Iowa, the Wisconsin, the Illinois and the great Missouri. In view of all the rain that had fallen, the Mississippi was relatively clear here. Islands of varying sizes dotted the river course, some of them not much more than bars of sandy mud rearing their heads, but others heavily overgrown with large trees and obviously permanent. The crossbreed's log, caught by the main current, did not approach any of them very closely.

Warmed to some degree by the early sun, the kitten became a little more animated, turning his head to watch the passing shoreline and once even raising a forepaw to the rim of the stub to lick it. Now and then he mewed pitifully.

Several times an impulse struck him to climb the rest of the way out of his branch and down to the narrow strip of log proper, but he became too afraid and did not attempt it. As stiff as his muscles were and as weak as he had become, the crossbreed might not be able to hold on; and if he should fall while climbing down the outside of the stub, chances were he would wind up in the water. Even were he successful in reaching that narrow arched section of the log still above water, what then? There was no place to go.

However uncomfortable his relatively secure position in the stub was, it was well for him that he did not leave it. The speed of the log gradually increased and then suddenly the log shot over the spillway of a small bunker dam just above the town of Alma.

For several minutes the log surged and rolled with the roaring current here, briefly turning upside down once and then, even after righting itself, continuing to wobble and spin about dizzyingly in the ripping currents and strong eddies. Had the little crossbreed followed his impulse and climbed out of the branch, he would have been lost.

Now, coughing and choking, soaking wet again and weak from both exposure and hunger, his head sagged and his eyes closed and once again he appeared more dead than alive. What's more, these times became more the rule than the exception, and by the middle of the morning he was only rarely raising his head or opening his eyes.

As a result, the kitten was not even aware of the small rowboat anchored ahead which the log was now rapidly approaching. A lone individual—a boy of about twelve—was sitting in the middle seat of the boat holding a fishing rod. Concentrating as he was on his angling, the boy did not become aware of the log until it actually began passing the boat about fifteen feet away.

He saw the kitten's head at once, immediately concluded it was dead and watched curiously as it floated past. But just then the little head rose and the eyes opened blearily. It was doubtful the young animal even saw the boy, for the eyes closed in just a few moments, and several seconds after that the head lolled and sank to rest on the forepaws.

The lad was not slow to react. He quickly reeled in his line and put his rod in the bottom of the boat. He then drew in his cord stringer upon which were tied a fair-sized bass and a smaller bluegill. These he also dropped on the floor of the boat where they flopped about furiously. By the time he pulled in the anchor, resumed his seat and took up the oars, the log was a hundred feet or more away, but this was no problem. With an expertness belying his age, the boy dipped his oars in sure strokes, and the boat sliced through the water in pursuit.

He overtook the log handily, ported his oars as he coasted the remaining few feet, then leaned out and gripped the stub just as the bow of the boat bumped heavily into the log. With an effort, the crossbreed raised his head and opened his eyes. At sight of the human, he made a feeble effort to snarl, but the sound that came out was a far cry from it. He tried to retreat deeper into the hollow, but his body simply wouldn't react quickly enough. A hand closed firmly over the scruff of his neck and carefully drew him forth. He managed to eke out a faint little hiss which brought a grin to the boy's face.

"Easy, li'l feller, easy," he said gently. "How'd you ever get stuck in there in the first place?"

On the seat beside the boy was a ragged terry-cloth towel he had brought along with which to wipe the slime from his hands after handling fish. It was slightly damp at one end, but this section he quickly tore off. Then he wrapped the remainder around the kitten until he was so well swaddled that only his head showed.

The lad held the bundle against himself firmly and, with his free hand, gently rubbed the kitten between the eyes. Under this ministration the little crossbreed's eyes closed. The boy opened his shirt front and stuffed the bundle inside, buttoned up and began rowing. They had drifted a fair distance downstream from where the boy had been anchored for fishing, but under his skillful handling they soon reached and passed that spot. They headed toward a wide, quiet creek mouth on the east bank of the river a mile or so below Alma and not very far above the mouth of the little Zumbro River of Minnesota, which entered the Mississippi from the west. As soon as the boat reached the more placid water in the expansive creek mouth and left the river current behind, the rowing was much easier, and they moved along smoothly for perhaps one hundred yards.

The creek then narrowed very rapidly and it became obvious that this was actually more of a river backwater than a large creek entering. The boy continued piloting the boat up the creek, now no more than twenty feet wide, for perhaps seventy yards more until they came to a sagging, poorly constructed wooden dock. It was really not much more than four old pilings connected by two-by-fours upon which some rough planking had been crudely nailed.

The boy tied the boat securely to one of the rotted pilings with the anchor rope, but he didn't get out immediately. Instead, he sat down again and withdrew the bulky bundle from his shirt. The crossbreed didn't appear very much improved in condition, and the boy shook his head.

"You're in sad shape, kitty-cat," he murmured. "Sure can't figure out how you come to get out there like that. From the looks of it, you been out there a good spell, too. Bet you're half starved."

He hooked the toe of his shoe around a bucket and drew it to him, reached in and, after a bit of fumbling, since there were only two left, withdrew a small minnow. He clenched his hand tightly over it until there was a faint pop as the air bladder broke and the fish was crushed. Then, with finger and thumb, he pinched off a chunk of meat about the size of a peanut. He held it in front of the crossbreed's nose.

"Here, try this."

Except to blink his eyes, the kitten didn't move. The boy shook his head again and rubbed the bit of fish against the animal's mouth. Instinctively the crossbreed licked his lips; hunger overruled fear and weakness and everything else. He snatched the morsel of fish from the fingers and gulped it down greedily, and the boy chuckled.

In a few minutes the entire fish had been eaten as individual bits handed to the kitten. The boy now returned his attention to the bucket where he swept his hand back and forth in an effort to catch the single minnow remaining. The little crossbreed, his eyes considerably brighter and more alert now, watched the boy's fumbling intently. In just these few elapsed minutes the food had worked wonders for him, and, though he made no effort to wriggle free of the towel still swaddled around him, there was little doubt that the crossbreed would survive.

A moment later, the boy grunted in triumph and withdrew his clenched hand, shook the excess water away and turned back to the kitten. He grinned when he saw how intently now the little eyes were following his movements.

"Huh. Looks like you were more hungry than anything else." He extended his arm and opened his wet hand just in front of the animal's nose. "Here's the last one. Want to try eatin' it whole?"

The exposed minnow lay gasping but quiescent in the middle of the boy's palm, and at once the kitten stretched out his head to get it. The little fish flopped the instant the kitten's nose touched it and dropped to the bottom of the boat where it flipped about in a frenzy. In catching the minnow again, the boy mashed it against the floor boards. This time, when he offered it to the kitten, there was no movement from the fish.

The little crossbreed was still too weak, however, to manage the whole minnow very well, and so once again the boy broke it into pieces between his fingers and fed him individual chunks of the white flesh. Again the kitten ate them eagerly and then licked the juices off the tips of the boy's fingers. Giggling at the sandpaper roughness of that tiny, pink tongue as it rasped across them, the boy held his fingers steady until the kitten was finished. Then he carefully tucked the towel and its contents under his arm, untied the stringer from the oarlock and stepped up onto the dilapidated dock which jiggled precariously.

"Guess the rod an' stuff'll be okay here till later on," the boy said. "I better get you up to the shed first thing an' see if I can sneak a little milk out of the house for you. Then maybe I can get you cleaned up some and see what you look like."

With the bass and bluegill—which had by this time expired—hanging close to the ground and the kitten tucked under the same arm, the boy picked his way through heavy underbrush along a narrow path which climbed a quickly steepening hill. Before long he was having to use his free hand to aid his progress and was actually doing more climbing than walking. By the time he reached a somewhat inclined plateau, he had climbed about sixty feet above the creek level and was panting a bit.

The path he was following now left the area of heavily wooded undercover and snaked diagonally through a sloping prairie toward an old, white frame house rather badly in need of both structural repair and painting. Thirty feet or more to one side stood the shed the boy had mentioned, which was in better condition than the small house. Between those two structures was parked a much dented and mud-bespattered auto some six or seven years old, its tires bald, its chrome and body rusted, and one headlight missing.

"Oh, oh," the boy murmured as he saw it, "Paw's home." He was obviously surprised at this and there was a distinct note of worry in his voice.

His father, Ed Andrews, hated cats with a passion, though his son never really knew why. What the boy did know of this aversion was enough to fill him now with a justifiable apprehension. He had seen his father deliberately run down several cats in the old car and shoot several others, including one that he killed with a .22 caliber rifle from the bedroom window that time when he spotted it slinking along behind the shed. The boy didn't know whether his father would act as unmercifully toward a helpless kitten, but he didn't care to chance it; he'd never had much feeling about those other cats one way or another, but he was suddenly determined that his new little charge would not meet a similar fate at his father's hands.

Becoming suddenly stealthy, he half crouched and angled off the path so that the shed remained between him and the house and he could approach unseen. Upon reaching the smaller structure, he sidled along the front of it to the narrow door, tripped the simple latch and slipped in, closing it quietly behind him.

Inside there was a jumble of junk material: a clutter of boxes tossed helter-skelter along the far wall in the rather dim interior; a heavy bench upon which were scattered a number of tools, many of which were broken and all of which were badly rusted; a large pile of old empty feed sacks; a few battered garden implements, including shovel, hoe, two old rakes with several teeth missing in each, and a five-pronged garden fork.

A cardboard carton that had once contained canned soup and was now half filled with yellowed newspapers and old magazines, rested on the floor beneath the single six-paned window which was so thick with dust it was difficult to see outside clearly. The boy nodded when he saw the box, dropped the two fish to the floor and then carefully placed the still-swaddled kitten down on one of the old sacks. He scooped up the papers and magazines from the carton and dumped them into another box partially filled with a conglomeration of metallic goods: an old corroded coffeepot, tin cans, a battered electric iron, a handleless iron skillet and other essentially worthless items.

He then shook a small cloud of dust out of three of the empty feed sacks and crammed them down into the bottom of the carton to make a soft warm flooring. A fourth sack he ripped open along the seams and spread out over the whole box. Carefully he pushed the center of this down until it rested on the other sacking and in such manner that the sides of the carton became roughly lined with the same material. He then gently placed the kitten and swaddling inside.

Though his hunger was far from appeased, the little crossbreed's head was sagging again. The warmth of his swaddling and the exhaustion of these many past hours had made an overpowering drowsiness spread through him, and his eyes closed. They opened briefly as the boy pulled a chunk of mud off his fur from between his ears, but then closed again. His ears and cheeks, in fact his entire head, was spattered with dried mud and, after studying his condition for a short while, the lad tiptoed to the door. He bent over and picked up the stringer with its two fish now stiff and dry on it, pulled them off and wrapped them in a sheet of the old newspaper. He slipped the door latch quietly and then glanced back at the soup carton.

"You wait here," he whispered, "and I'll be right back."

The door closed and the latch clicked quietly back into place, but the slumbering kitten did not even move.

VI

Todd Andrews sauntered with exaggerated casualness toward the house, carrying his newspaper-wrapped fish. When he entered the kitchen, he forgot for the hundredth time the strong spring and winced as the screen door banged shut loudly behind him.

"Todd!" His mother's voice was sharp but not as angry as he'd expected. "What've I told you about letting the door slam like that?"

"Sorry, Maw," he called. "Didn't mean to. It kind'a slipped a little."

"Seems like that door does a lot of slipping when you go in and out, young man. Well, all right. Come in here a minute. Your father's home and he wants to tell you something."

"Be right there." The boy tossed the newspaper package onto a shelf in the ancient, badly chipped refrigerator and closed that door quietly. Then he shrugged out of his light jacket, hung it over the broom closet doorknob and went into the living room. He was very surprised to see his father dressed in his rather seedy suit and even more so to see the big twin-strapped imitation leather suitcase, bulging slightly with its contents, standing on the floor beside the front door.

The elder Andrews was hardly a striking individual. He was rather short and lean and had somewhat of a harried look about him. He was bald across the front third of his head and his eyes were a washed-out gray. He looked to be about forty years old and appeared ill at ease dressed in this manner. As Todd approached him, the man stuck out his hand and smiled at him.

"Well, boy," he said, "shake hands. I'm gonna be leavin' here for a spell."

"Leaving?" Todd was perplexed. The last time Paw had gone anywhere was a year ago last February when he had attended the national duck-calling contest at the Sportsmen's Show in Chicago. It was a contest he might well have won, since he was an excellent caller, but he had forfeited his opportunity by getting gloriously drunk and then trying to play "Yankee Doddle" on the duck call when his turn came. Todd reached out his own small hand, took the rather bony one extended to him and shook it dutifully, then asked his father where he was going.

"Got me a job, boy," Ed Andrews said proudly. "Mister Jeffers, he liked the way I helped set up the new 'quipment at his shop so well that he fixed things for me to work for 'im at the new place he just bought down at St. Louie. Tol' me I got a natural bent, as he called it, for motors an' machinery an' suchlike. That's what he said."

Maude Andrews slipped an arm about her son's shoulders and hugged him. She was a pleasant-appearing woman with a touch of gray in her black hair. It was easy to see that Todd had inherited his well-formed features from her, even though his sandy-colored hair and gray eyes apparently came from his father's side. She hugged Todd to her briefly and her smile was a worried one.

"Your father's going to be gone for three or four months, Toddy," she said, then added after a brief pause, "and maybe, if things work out good, he'll get the job permanent, and we can go down there to live."

She was smiling, but the boy could see she was close

to tears and he guessed she was scared that Paw would ruin it all again by getting himself all liquored up.

"How's come, Paw?" he asked, frowning. "I mean, how's come you just don't stay here an' work for Mister Jeffers?"

"Ain't got no choice," his father said rather irritably. "The job I done for him here is done, an' they ain't no other work. I'm lucky he wants me to go down there, boy. He's even payin' my train fare. You know I ain't had steady work for a right good spell, an' we ain't able to pick an' choose. Gotta take what we get. Mebbe, like your ma says, this'll work out into somethin' permanent."

Todd blinked and smiled, but he knew his mother was thinking the same thoughts as he. His father's words were not unfamiliar, even though the circumstances were. How many times in the past had he started some job here in Alma or Cochrane or a few of the other nearby towns with the speculation that maybe it'd work into something permanent? And how many times had it fallen through because of the same old problem?

They continued talking as the elder Andrews made a final check to see that he had everything he would need. Then the suitcase was tossed into the back seat of the car, and Todd's mother and father got in. She rolled down the window on her side and waved her fingers at Todd who stood on the back porch.

"I've got some shopping to do in Winona after I see your father off at the station," she said. "I'll be back in a few hours. There's some wieners in the ice box, and you can eat them for your lunch. Be a good boy now and stay close to home."

He nodded. "Okay, Maw. Be careful. 'Bye, Paw. And Paw . . ." he hesitated, ". . . good luck."

Ed Andrews flushed, and Todd immediately regretted saying it. Both of them knew what he meant. He braced himself for the expected flare-up of his father's temper and he saw his mother's lips pinch together as she frowned at him. His father leaned over her to talk out of her window, but apparently he chose to interpret Todd's meaning another way.

"Luck ain't got nothin' t'do with it, boy," he replied expansively. "Skill, that's what. That's why Mister Jeffers is sendin' me down there. He's got a job t'be done an' I can do it an' he knows it. Ain't no luck about it. You take care of your ma now while I'm gone, hear? An' you mind what she says, too, hear?"

"Yessir, Paw, I will. 'Bye."

"So long, boy."

His father said something else, but it was lost in the loud grinding of the starter. Then the car lurched forward. His mother waved to him again, and he waved back, and then they were gone, bumping and squeaking down the badly rutted road leading toward Route 35 which would take them down about twenty-five miles to Bluff Siding. That was where they'd cross over the big bridge to Winona, Minnesota.

Todd Andrews was thoughtful as he went back into the house and opened the door of the ancient, scarred refrigerator. He wished that just once his father would call him "son" or "Todd" rather than "boy" as he always did. He shook his head sadly. He'd really meant it when he wished his father good luck. Despite the way he sometimes treated Maw and him, he was a good man, and Todd, in a reserved and often rather frightened sort of way, loved him. Especially for Maw's sake he wanted him to make out well on the new job. It might be the turning point of their lives if he did. And he could, too, if he'd just stay away from the liquor.

Todd sighed deeply and inspected the refrigerator shelves without much interest. There wasn't a great deal inside: a few covered dishes with leftovers in them, a cellophane package containing a dozen wieners, half a head of cabbage, a package of some kind of meat rolled in butcher's paper. There was also, beside the newspaper-wrapped fish, a half gallon of milk.

The latter items stirred him. The kitten! He'd forgotten all about it in the surprise of his father's departure and now he snatched the jug of milk and set it on the table. He clattered about in a cupboard beside the sink, took out a small pan, filled it three-fourths full of milk and put it on the range to warm.

Then he got a clean scrub bucket out of the broom closet, put it into the sink and half filled it with warm water. He shoved a small bar of white soap into his pocket, and by that time the milk was lightly steaming. He turned off the fire, poured the pan's contents into a large bowl and then carried bucket and bowl to the screen door, which he shouldered open. With a mischievous little smile, he allowed it to slam loudly behind him and then walked to the shed.

He placed the bucket on the ground and opened the shed door gently. One of the kitten's ears twitched at the sound, but the little crossbreed did not open his eyes or raise his head. Todd set the bucket inside, shut the door and then put the bowl of milk on the floor beside the carton.

The kitten awoke when he was lifted and protested weakly as the boy unwrapped him. A faint growl escaped his throat and the boy laughed aloud, dropped the towel to the floor and then stood the little animal beside the bowl. At once the aroma of the warm milk touched the crossbreed's nostrils and he became more alert. Apparently, however, he did not know how to go about drinking milk from a bowl. He hunched a little when Todd pushed the bowl over so that it was just below his face, but still he didn't drink.

Gently the lad forced the kitten's head down until the end of his snout was in the milk and then he released him. The little crossbreed's head rose and he licked his lips automatically. The taste of the milk excited him considerably, and when again the boy put a little pressure at the back of his head, he didn't balk but lowered his face and began lapping.

It was that simple.

At first the little tongue flicked out and in with great rapidity, but gradually, as the level of the fluid lowered, it slowed. At last, with still a half-inch of milk left in the bottom of the bowl, the little animal could drink no more. His stomach bulged ludicrously and practically touched the floor beneath him.

He licked his lips and yawned widely; and now, for the first time since coming in contact with this boy, he neither flinched nor showed any indication of fear or anger as the hands reached out and carefully picked him up. That newfound sense of security did not last long. The boy had discovered a large, badly dented roasting pan in a box on the other side of the room. Now, instead of putting the kitten back into the bed carton, he placed him in the pan, holding him down with one hand while, with the other, he scooped a couple of canfuls of warm water from the bucket and poured them into the pan.

At the first touch of the water the little crossbreed became panicky and began to yowl with unexpected loudness. It was the first really significant sound he'd made since the boy had rescued him. Suddenly, he was spitting and scratching and struggling to get free, but Todd had been expecting some reaction like this; he had a good grip on the kitten and held him tightly against the pan. As the prolonged yowls continued, he crooned soothingly and then kept up a running line of talk as he took the soap from his pocket and began to wash the badly muddied animal.

"Y'know," he said, "not long ago I read a book from the school library 'bout a big dog called Old Yeller. Reckon they called him that 'cause of his color, but maybe partly 'cause of the big voice he had when he barked. Well, I'll tell you something, kitty-cat, for a little feller you got an awful big voice, too. Know what I'm gonna call you? I'm gonna name you Old Yowler."

He chuckled at his play on words and continued washing the kitten. The little crossbreed had given up struggling and now merely stood there shivering uncontrollably as the suds were massaged into his fur and the water became a light chocolate brown. Once, when Todd's fingers came close to his mouth as he washed his head, the kitten made a halfhearted attempt to bite him, but was unsuccessful.

Todd clucked his tongue in admonition. He looked reflectively at the soaked animal and then amended his decision of a few moments ago.

"No, don't reckon I can call you Old Yowler, 'cause you sure ain't very old, but the second part fits you fine. From now on, little feller, your name is Yowler. How's that?"

He continued chattering away until at last the washing was finished. Then he picked up the little crossbreed and held him down in the bucket until just his head was out of the water, massaging the fur with his free hand and rinsing away the soap and grime. Once again the panic returned, and the crossbreed gave vent to another spate of the frightened yowling. The cry grew in intensity immediately after the boy had momentarily ducked the kitten's head beneath the surface, but then it became muffled as the towel, in which he had been wrapped before, was again wrapped around him and he was rubbed briskly.

"Yep," the boy said cheerfully, "Yowler it is."

Todd was careful to dry the little crossbreed thoroughly. When he had finished, the animal's fur was fluffy and very soft and quite attractively marked. And then, though he'd been handling the kitten for some time now, the boy first noticed that there was no tail, or at least not much of one.

His first thought was that the kitten had lost it somehow and he studied the short appendage carefully. Suddenly his eyes widened and his mouth gaped. He quickly inspected the ears and then also noticed for the first time that the hairs at the tips of them were quite long and dark and showed promise of becoming even longer. These ears were most definitely going to be peaked. Other items about the little crossbreed's appearance now took on a new meaning: his coloration, his wildness, the size of his feet and the length of his legs.

"Holy mackerel!" Todd breathed. "You're a bobcat, Yowler. An honest-to-goodness bobcat!"

Momentarily the boy's eyes danced with the excitement of his discovery and then he frowned and shook his head as he placed the kitten back into the carton and covered him snugly with a folded section of one of the old feed sacks. He rubbed the little crossbreed's ears soothingly and massaged the back of the furry neck.

"Boy, all I can say is it's a good thing for both of us Paw's gone," he muttered. "Ain't hardly no doubt he'd kill you an' prob'ly half kill me to boot. Maw, now, she's another matter. Know what she'll say? She'll say, 'Todd! Have you lost your senses? You can't keep that animal here. You know how your father hates cats!' Then, when she sees you're a bobcat, she'll have even more of a fit. But you know what? Soon as she gets a good look at you an' I let 'er hold you a little—an' listen, Yowler, when I do, don't you put up no fuss, hear? You scratch or bite her an' you'll fix it good for both of us. Anyhow, like I was sayin', when she gets to hold you an' sees how cute you are, she'll give in an' say I can keep you 'til Paw comes home. An' when he *does* get here . . . well, we'll worry about that later."

The little crossbreed was asleep again; the fresh cleanliness and warmth, the stomachful of warm milk and the caressing touch of the boy had made an over-powering drowsiness close in upon him again. It was a very sound sleep, and yet the boy detected a faint vibration as his fingertips rubbed the fur. He put his head close to the little animal and very faintly, but unmistakably, he heard it.

The little crossbreed was purring.

VII

The reaction of Maude Andrews to the kitten was amazingly close to that predicted by her son, even to the conversation they would have. At first she was strong in her declaration that the animal would have to go, but the very helplessness of the little creature melted her resistance. And when, the day after his father had gone away, Todd encouraged her to hold the kitten and feed it a little cube of flesh he had cut from one of his fish, she was won over.

She wondered aloud how such a little kitten had lost its tail, and Todd, fearful that her mood might change, merely shrugged and did not tell her what he believed to be true, that this was a bobcat, not a common house cat.

For his own part, the little crossbreed adapted to his new life extremely well. Undoubtedly he came to look forward to Todd's visits, which were frequent and prolonged, and yet for a long while he couldn't completely shake off the instinctive feeling of alarm and fear when the boy's hand would reach out to stroke his fur or pick him up.

During those first few weeks he was perfectly content

to remain in the shed and amuse himself. He prowled about with progressively less awkwardness through the clutter of boxes and tools and occasionally batted about, or rolled over and over with the golf-ball-sized tuft of bright red yarn Todd had brought for him.

One day the boy sat on the shed floor with the little crossbreed in his lap, stroking him gently. Both kitten and youngster fell asleep. Sometime later, the boy felt his pet stiffen in his grasp and begin trembling faintly. He opened his eyes.

The little bobtail was tapping nervously against his hand as it flicked back and forth in erratic little jerks. Todd's gaze followed the intent stare of the kitten and immediately locked on the same thing the crossbreed had seen.

Apparently oblivious to the presence of anyone else, a small field mouse had poked its head out from between two boxes and then emerged entirely and began moving purposefully toward a crust of bread lying on the floor not far from the soup-carton bed—a bit of food that the little crossbreed had scorned when Todd brought it to him.

When the mouse was about halfway to the bread, the kitten sprang into action. Leaping from Todd's lap, he covered the distance between himself and mouse in two bounds. It was one bound too many.

Instantly perceiving its peril, the mouse sped off to one side on the kitten's first jump and neatly dodged the next leap. Before the little crossbreed could recover, the rodent had disappeared between the boxes again, and though the kitten sniffed anxiously about the clutter and clambered over the boxes, the mouse was nowhere to be found.

"You're gonna have to do better'n that, Yowler," said Todd. "You jumped way too soon. If you'd've waited a while, that ol' mouse would've prob'ly come close enough for you to grab."

The little crossbreed, reluctantly giving up the search, trotted back to the boy and hunched his back luxuriously as the lad scratched him. Todd picked him up and held him on his lap so that the kitten was facing him.

"One of these days, little feller, Paw'll be coming back, and then who knows what'll happen?" The boy continued, "Maybe he'll let me keep you, but then again, maybe he'll make me turn you loose. If he does, then you better know how to hunt, 'cause there won't be nobody to bring you food no more. Guess if you were still livin' with your maw wherever you were born, she'd be teachin' you how to hunt. An', since I'm sort'a takin' her place, I reckon we better get down to business an' give you some lessons."

He set the little crossbreed on the floor. The kitten watched him curiously as he searched in his pockets and drew forth a six-foot length of old fishing line. Todd tied the line to the ball of yarn and then stuffed the ball into the little crack between two boxes, the same two boxes from which the mouse had initially emerged.

He stretched the string out until it was fully extended and then he placed the kitten at the spot where the loose line ended. Curious, the little crossbreed wanted to walk around, but Todd stopped him, gently but firmly holding him to the floor so that the kitten had to lie on his stomach. Twice, as he eased the pressure of his hand, the little crossbreed tried to rise, and twice Todd forced him back into place. The third time he relaxed his pressure; the kitten stayed put.

"Now watch, Yowler," the boy said. "We've got to pretend that that there piece of fuzz is a mouse, okay? And when a mouse comes out, you can't just right away jump up and run after him, see? You got to have patience and wait 'til he's close."

He pulled the string and, as it tightened, the kitten's eyes narrowed and he watched it with interest. The line stretched, held for a moment, and then the ball of yarn abruptly popped from the crack and rolled to a stop nine or ten inches out on the open floor.

Instantly the little crossbreed's muscles flexed and he attempted to jump after it, but the hand on his back pressed him to the floor again and the voice of the boy came soothingly.

"No, no, Yowler, not yet. You got to wait. Now see, that's a mouse an' he doesn't see you yet and you got to wait till he comes closer. Watch close now."

With his free hand he pulled the line in little jerks and spurts as well as steady pulls of about a foot. Several times more the kitten tried to get up, but still Todd held him down until at last the ball of fluff had been drawn to within two feet. Then, instead of holding him, the boy pushed the kitten forward and the little crossbreed leaped through the air and pounced upon the "mouse." He rolled over with it roughly, biting it and scratching at it with his sharp little hind claws.

Todd let him enjoy himself for a little while with the lure and then he took it away, hid it at another point and repeated the entire process. Throughout the afternoon he continued the training, and the little crossbreed actually seemed to revel in it. By the time they had done it a half-dozen times, it was no longer necessary for Todd to keep Yowler from jumping up too soon.

Distinctly pleased with the little crossbreed for so quickly understanding what was expected of him, Todd now tried a different maneuver. With care, he positioned the yarn ball so that it was in sight, but when he pulled on the line, it disappeared around the box. The kitten, very interested, prepared to jump after it again, but the boy told him no several times, pressing him to the floor each time, until the little crossbreed realized he was meant to stay where he was.

Then Todd put him across the room where he could see both the ball, after it disappeared from Todd's sight around the box, and the boy. Getting down on his hands and knees, Todd pretended he had just spied the prey and instantly he crouched until his chin was almost at floor level. With his concealed hand he tugged on the string, and the ball scooted around the corner of the box and stopped out of his view. The boy, seeing Yowler's muscles bunch, whispered "No!" and the kitten remained poised where he was.

Raising and lowering each hand slowly and quietly in turn, Todd crept forward, pausing often and pretending to sniff the scent of his prey in the air. It was a remarkably adept burlesque of the stalking the little crossbreed's mother had done of the snowshoe rabbit shortly before the flood, and now the kitten gazed intently at the boy.

At last, when Todd was just around the corner of the box from this "mouse," he abruptly spurted forward, reached out and snatched up the ball and crammed it into his mouth, growling ferociously.

The excited kitten pranced over to him. At once Todd spit out the fluff, and the little crossbreed pounced on it in turn, while Todd laughed happily. It was as much sport for the boy as it was for the animal. The principle of this type of hunting, involving stalking as well as patience, was a bit more difficult for the kitten to grasp, and it was four days before he fully realized what was expected of him and what he should do.

Todd, with the skill of a natural-born teacher, never became impatient with him, although on one or two occasions when the little crossbreed became overexcited and broke too soon, he cuffed him sharply enough to bowl him over, but not hard enough to hurt him. He was immensely pleased with Yowler's progress, and gradually the lessons became even more involved and required more of the pupil.

He would position the bait and move it out of sight and watch with delight as the little animal flattened his ears against his head and crept forward to the crucial point. Then, as the kitten sprang to the attack, he would jerk the ball away as if it were trying to flee. The first few times the fluff succeeded in escaping, but before long, no matter how rapidly or erratically he was jerking it away, the little crossbreed followed and caught it.

The day when the kitten obviously began thinking for himself and planning his strategy was a day that filled Todd with a glow of pride. He had positioned the fluff ball as usual so that it could be drawn around the box, but this time, when it disappeared past the corner and out of sight of Yowler, the kitten did not follow. Instead, Yowler ran forward rapidly in a crouching posture at the opposite direction around the box. At the back corner he sank to the floor and poised, tail twitching. Taken aback but distinctly pleased, Todd continued to pull the ball of fluff until it appeared at that corner of the box. Instantly the little crossbreed pounced onto it and bit it sharply.

Little by little, as more days and weeks passed, the training progressed, and reflexes and cunning of the kitten sharpened amazingly. The pair had become virtually inseparable and by the end of six weeks the little crossbreed was following Todd everywhere, more like a little dog than a cat. Frequently he stood on the shore of the creek below the prairie and watched as the boy seined up minnows to use as bait in his fishing; always Todd tossed a lively, wriggling little fish to him, and he would catch it deftly while it was still in the air, end its life with a quick bite of the head and then devour it.

Quite often they went out fishing in the little rowboat together and, though at first the little crossbreed was afraid, he soon realized that he was safe in the boat with Todd. He showed great interest each time a fish was caught, devouring eagerly the small flopping bluegills the boy tossed to him and watching with what seemed to be disappointment as the larger bluegills and bass were put on a stringer and lowered back into the water.

He had grown remarkably in these weeks. By no means yet full size, his body was already as large as an adult house cat's and he was considerably taller. His ear tufts had by this time become attractively peaked and the fur on his cheeks had also become decidedly tufted. Even though the pattern of his markings was not quite right for a bobcat—a fact that more than once caused

Todd to frown in puzzlement—there could be little doubt that this was no ordinary cat.

When it had become apparent that Yowler would not run off, even when unattended, Todd had, with some difficulty, raised the shed's single six-paned window about a foot, and since it had no sash weights, propped it open with a section of the broom handle. He placed an old nail keg outside under the window, and now the young crossbreed could enter or leave whenever he was so inclined. Still, the young cat had shown no desire to leave his new home, and Todd's initial trepidation at permitting him his freedom of movement soon vanished.

They had long since graduated from the early days of training with the ball of yarn fluff, and Todd did his best to continue the kitten's training in the field. Together they prowled along the numerous rabbit and mouse trails in the big prairie, Todd often crawling along on hands and knees.

Early in this outside training they found the well-concealed nest of a meadowlark deep in the prairie grasses. Within it were four newly hatched young. Although normally the boy would not have bothered them, now he let Yowler have his way with them.

The young crossbreed caught scent of the baby birds before he saw them, and instinctively he hugged the ground and crept forward toward the nest until he was no more than ten inches from it. Then he pounced. The boy nodded in approval as he saw how Yowler bunched the whole of the nest within his grasp to prevent the escape of the parent bird, should it be there. It was not and so the crossbreed tore the nest to shreds and devoured the four small nestlings.

This was his first living, warmblooded meat, and a subtle change came over him as he ate. He seemed strangely fiercer and more a creature of the wild than a pet. He growled faintly as he ate, and when he had finished and Todd had made a slight movement toward him, he started and flinched as if he had forgotten the boy was even there. For just an instant before he caught himself, his ears moved flat against his head and his lip curled in the beginning of a snarl.

Taken slightly aback at this unexpected change in character, Todd murmured softly at him and rubbed his back; in a moment the wild animal was once again the tame young cat. A deep purring rumbled from his chest and he arched his back at the exquisite enjoyment of the boy's stroking hand.

On another day Todd led the crossbreed to a small pile of boards which he began turning over. It was a heyday of activity for the animal, because beneath nearly every board there was something. Crickets and beetles jumped or scurried to get back into cover, and by the time all but one piece of material—a wide strip of weathered plywood—had been tossed to one side, he had caught and eaten one or two of the black beetles and a half dozen large crickets.

As the piece of plywood was overturned, the crossbreed was ready and sprang forward at once, pouncing upon a ball-like nest of grasses as if he not only knew it was going to be there, but its precise location as well. A piercing little squeal came from the nest, and the crossbreed's muzzle dipped down and then came up with a mouthful of the grass in which a large meadow mouse was struggling. Her struggles ceased abruptly as the young cat's teeth bit deeply. She had the dubious honor of being the first mouse the crossbreed had ever caught.

Without pause the crossbreed dropped her and returned his attention to the nest. There was a minor riot of activity as he found and slew five newly furred baby mice. Then he sat on his haunches and commenced eating them.

"Boy-oh-boy, Yowler," Todd said approvingly, "you're really a hunter now, ain't you? Don't reckon there's much more I can teach you. Y'know, maybe when Paw comes home an' he sees how well you catch mice, he won't mind having you around." He spoke hopefully but without much conviction.

He knew his father too well.

VIII

However well Todd Andrews knew his father, he didn't even begin to anticipate the man's reaction to the young crossbreed. At the end of the tenth week after his departure, Ed Andrews returned in the middle of the afternoon. He was decidedly drunk. He was also very loud but nearly incoherent in his diatribe against a "miser'ble boss" who'd fired him merely because he'd taken a little nip to "fight off a cold."

When Todd, without any trace or intent of insolence in his question, asked him what had happened, his father stared blearily at him for a moment and then, without any warning, lashed out and slapped him so hard that the boy lost his footing and fell against a rocking chair. Both he and the rocker tumbled to the floor.

"You just mind your own business, boy!" his father snarled. "I aim t'see to it that you ain't gonna be like the rest of 'em, stickin' their noses in other folks' affairs."

Maude Andrews gasped and helped the boy to his feet. Then, her eyes flashing angrily, she spun around to confront her husband.

"Ed, for heaven's sake, what's *wrong* with you? You got no call to hit Toddy like that. Just because you can't keep away from the—" She caught herself suddenly, squeezed Todd's shoulder and tried to smile but failed. "Todd, honey, you run out and leave us alone here for a little while, huh?"

Todd had been too stunned even to cry out at the blow he had received and now he stumbled from the room and ran to the shed. He picked Yowler up and sat on the floor, holding him in his lap. And then the tears came, tears inspired as much by the hot argument he could hear faintly coming from inside the house as by the slap which inflamed his cheek. The young crossbreed licked Todd's face and fingers and then curled in his lap and promptly fell asleep. The boy sat there sobbing for a long while.

Toward evening he returned to the house and found that his mother had gotten his father into bed; late that night, in his own bedroom, Todd awakened to hear the muffled sound of their voices in argument again, and after a while he knew his mother was crying. Even though he wasn't sure exactly why, a rush of tears came to his own eyes and he groaned softly and buried his head under his pillow.

The next morning, as they sat bleakly around the breakfast table, there was little conversation. Maude Andrews was tight-lipped and red-eyed and Todd's father was surly and in an ugly mood. The boy knew this, of all times, was no time to bring up the subject of Yowler. The confidence he had tried to instill in himself over the past few weeks about his father's acceptance of the animal simply drained away. He knew now what he had been trying all along to deny to himself, that his father would never accept even a regular house cat, much less a bobcat.

The boy sat there, picking disinterestedly at his fried mush, wondering what he should do now. He didn't have much time to consider the problem. He happened to glance out of the window toward the shed, and there, casually licking a paw, Yowler sat upon the nail keg beneath his window. Todd sucked in his breath in an involuntary gasp.

Ed Andrews looked sharply at his son and then followed the line of the boy's gaze out the window. With an exclamation he dropped his fork and leaped up from the table so abruptly that he overturned his chair. He ran out of the room and a moment later charged back with his rifle and clattered out onto the back porch, Todd at his heels and Maude Andrews close behind them both.

"No, Paw, no!" Todd yelled as the man stopped and leveled the rifle. "Don't shoot, Paw! That's Yowler. He's mine. I raised him, Paw, he's a pet. *Please, Paw, please—don't shoot him!*"

He tugged at his father's arm, but the man cursed and thrust him away savagely and once again brought the rifle to bear. The young crossbreed, startled by this outburst on the porch, stood up. The man was strange to him, and his hackles raised slightly as he sensed his peril. Once before he had seen an object similar to the one being pointed at him by this man, and that was the time he had witnessed the death of his bobcat sire. Fear suddenly flooding him, he leaped off the keg, and at that moment the rifle cracked.

There was a terrifying spanging sound as the slug hit the metal crossband of the keg and ricocheted viciously away with a quickly diminishing whine. The crossbreed hit the ground running and sped around the corner of the shed just as the rifle cracked again and another bullet tore into the edge of the building. The wood splintered and a small sharp piece hit his shoulder and stuck deeply there. He ran as he had never run before.

Behind him he could hear loud voices and cries, but there were no more shots. Soon even those sounds faded as he raced deeper into the woods, following the creek bank upstream. For five minutes he ran and then he stopped behind a large moldering log and listened intently.

He heard nothing.

His legs and sides were trembling, and his tail flicked back and forth almost uncontrollably. The pain in his shoulder was more evident now that he had stopped running, and he bent his head around and managed to get his teeth on the projecting bit of wood. However, he could not get the necessary leverage or pulling distance, and after several unsuccessful tries at pulling the splinter loose, he gave up.

Although the fear was still strong in him, the initial panic was gone. He lay down close to the log, more relaxed now but still ready for instant flight should it become necessary. His shoulder throbbed some, but the wound was actually more painful than serious.

Yowler didn't know what to do, and so for the next quarter hour he merely stayed where he was, occasionally licking his wound, his ears twitching at every sound. At last there came a distant call which caused him to stand erect and cock his head. It had sounded like the voice of the boy. He listened intently but heard nothing further.

Limping slightly now, he padded toward the edge of the woods and there, screened by undergrowth, he looked across the sloping prairie at the house and shed, perhaps a quarter of a mile away. There was no sign of life about either, and he was tempted to go back there, since the shed had been his home and place of security.

His wild heritage, however, overruled this inclination and instead he moved back into the woods toward the creek. A short distance farther up the bank he found where a tree had fallen, creating a natural bridge over the stream. He walked across and then paused to listen on the other side.

Again the sound came to him, and now there was no mistaking it; the boy was calling him from somewhere downstream. At once he began following this far shore in that direction. He was still fifty yards or more above the rickety little pier when he heard the boy's voice very distinctly.

"Yowler . . . *Yowler!*" The call was low, but intense. "Yowler, where are you? I won't hurt you, boy. Please,

Yowler, come back. Paw's up at the house. I won't let him hurt you. *Yowler!*"

A faint sound welled in the crossbreed's throat. Across the creek and halfway down the steep bank he could see occasional glimpses of the boy as Todd stumbled and slithered down through the heavy brush. His calling ceased as he strove to keep himself from falling, but when he reached more level ground a short distance from the pier, he called again.

The crossbreed stepped into a clearing along the shore and gave voice to a penetrating yowl. Todd heard it and stopped in his tracks. He looked all around anxiously.

"Yowler? Yowler, it's me. I won't hurt you. Where are you?"

The young cat limped along the shore toward the boy, and then Todd saw him across the creek. Relief and anxiety were evident in his voice.

"Yowler! Oh, Yowler, you didn't run away, did you? I thought I'd never see you again." For the first time he saw that the crossbreed was limping slightly and he sucked in his breath. "You're hurt! I thought Paw missed you, but you're hurt. Wait there."

He ran to the dock and untied the little wooden boat, jumped in and rapidly rowed across. The low, whining sound in the crossbreed's throat continued as the old craft approached, and his tail flicked expectantly a few times. As the prow of the boat neared shore, he bunched and then leaped into it. At once the boy dropped his oars and scooped the animal up in his arms. His voice was shaky and tears streamed from his eyes.

"Oh, Yowler, I'm sorry, I'm so sorry," he sniffled. "I should'a known that was what Paw'd do. I should'a known."

The young crossbreed licked Todd's hands and then his chin, his own body wriggling enthusiastically at the reunion. The low, pleased sound continued to roll from deep within his throat.

After a few moments the boy's fingers began exploring gently through the fur of the crossbreed's leg for the wound. When he inadvertently brushed against the splinter, the cat flinched. Puzzled, Todd spread the hairs and saw the bit of wood projecting. He touched it softly with a fingertip and, though the crossbreed winced a little, he did not pull away. The boy's voice was relieved.

"Not a bullet hole after all, Yowler. I was scared you'd been hit. You must've run into a piece of board or something. Now you hold still"—he gripped the end of the bit of wood firmly between thumb and index finger —" 'cause this'll prob'ly hurt a little."

He gave a sharp yank and pulled it free, but the crossbreed didn't even move. He held up the splinter for the cat to see and then pitched it into the water. As the crossbreed began licking the wound, Todd stroked his back.

"Got nothing to put on it for you, Yowler," he said, "but I guess it ain't so very bad anyhow. Day or two, an' it ought'a be like new again. By then we'll be a good long ways from here. You an' me, we're gonna make out just fine." The boat had pulled away from the shore and was drifting very lazily toward the wider backwater mouth of the creek, and Todd smiled. "Leastways we won't go hungry. Soon as we start drifting good on the river, we'll see what we can catch."

With his toe he nudged the old fishing rod which lay in the bottom of the boat. Beside it was a small canvas bag in which he kept extra hooks and other fishing paraphernalia, along with several boxes of matches. There was also a paper sack under the seat which contained an apple and a stale sandwich wrapped in waxed paper which he had left there two days ago. They were pitifully few supplies with which to embark upon the sort of journey the boy was envisioning, but that didn't concern him in the least.

Bending to the oars, Todd rowed smoothly into the wider waters of the creek mouth and then well out into the open waters of the Mississippi River. Perhaps fifty yards from shore, where the current was moving well, he ported the oars and once again took the young crossbreed into his lap and stroked him.

They sat quietly, watching the shoreline slip past, and as they drifted by the foot of the bluff behind which his house lay, tears filled Todd's eyes again. Though he made no sound, the tears dribbled down his cheeks and off his chin rather copiously for a while. Finally, more than a mile from where they had left the creek, the river curved, and the high bluffs with which he was so familiar disappeared from sight.

The young crossbreed leaned against his chest and purred, his fears almost gone now. Content to be close to his young protector, his eyes all but closed and he very nearly fell asleep. Todd looked down at him and smiled, then rubbed his own nose into the soft fur between the animal's ears.

Even now the boy wasn't giving much thought to their destination, but he didn't much care. The main concern was to get Yowler out of the reach of his father, and in this he was succeeding admirably. Thought of his father—and then of his mother—caused a slight frown to wrinkle his forehead, and a delayed shudder from his previous crying shook his chest. His eyes began to fill again, but then he shook his head.

"Paw won't care I'm gone, Yowler," he muttered. "Don't reckon he much cares about anything 'cept himself. Not for me, that's for sure, and I guess not even a whole awful lot for Maw. He'll prob'ly be glad I'm gone, 'cause then he won't haft'a be bothered with me."

The crossbreed's ears twitched as the boy talked, but his eyes were closed now and the rumbling purr continued without break. Another frown creased the boy's forehead.

"And Maw . . . well, Maw knows I can take care of myself. Anyway, she's got her hands full enough with Paw." He paused for a long while, thinking about her, and his chin began trembling. He buried his face deeper into the fur of the crossbreed's scruff, and his words became muffled. "Hope she won't worry very much about me."

But he knew she would.

IX

Throughout the day they drifted.

It was a pleasant day, warm and bright, and it was interesting for Todd to see the unfamiliar shoreline sliding past, to wave back at the occasional people on shore or in other boats who waved at him.

At the low Mississippi River dams numbered five and six, located at Whitman and Lamoille, they portaged, the crossbreed prancing about on shore at such times, no longer limping from his slight shoulder wound. Meanwhile Todd, grunting and puffing, dragged the small boat around the concrete obstructions.

In the early afternoon Todd became hungry and so he opened the paper bag and took out the sandwich and apple. The bread was stiff and dry and the peanut butter between the slices was very gummy. Nevertheless, he munched it appreciatively and offered a chunk to the crossbreed who sniffed it eagerly at first, but then turned his back on it and resumed the position he most favored when they were in the boat—curled up on the small seat in the prow.

Feeling guilty at having something to eat for himself, but nothing for Yowler, the boy rigged up his fishing outfit immediately after eating all but a small piece of the bread. This morsel he moistened with saliva and then rolled into a tight ball about the size of a marble. He baited his hook with it, dropped it over the side and let the line drift along in the current with the boat. Then he began to eat the apple.

He had just finished the fruit and tossed the core away when he felt something on his line. There was a faint nudge at first and then a long powerful run as something streaked away with the bread bait. He let it go for twenty or thirty feet and then set the hook hard. At once the rod bucked in his grip and bent in a tight arc. He fought the fish well until the last few moments when he got it to the surface near the boat and saw that it was a large carp, weighing easily twelve pounds or more.

"Hey, you're gonna eat like a king, Yowler," he chortled, dragging the fish toward him.

The crossbreed was standing on the front seat watching the battle with lively interest. But Todd now became too eager. The fish was not yet played out, and when he pulled it close beside the boat and reached his hand out for it, the carp gave a sudden powerful surge and the fishing line snapped just above the hook. Dejected, Todd stared at the water where the fish had disappeared and then kicked angrily at his tackle bag.

"My own fault," he grumbled. "Should'a took more time. Now we're gonna have to dig some bait. You prob'ly want to stretch your muscles some anyway, don't you, Yowler?"

The crossbreed licked his lips, and Todd laughed at him and then began rowing toward the steeply banked east shore. The instant the keel of the boat rubbed against the bottom, the crossbreed leaped to his feet. When the craft ground to a stop several feet from the shoreline on a gravelly bar, Todd ported his oars, stepped out into the water and shoved the boat well up where it would be secure from drifting away. At once the crossbreed jumped out and began running around, sniffing eagerly among rocks and driftwood. Almost immediately he startled a small leopard frog which leaped in a great arc toward the water, but the crossbreed pounced on him as he landed and ate him at once.

Todd was also exploring the shore, and after several minutes he picked up a rusted tin can and then set about climbing the steep bank while the young crossbreed was still eating his catch. When Todd was nearly at the top, he looked down and saw that the young cat had finished eating and was beginning to follow him upward. He yelled, "C'mon, Yowler!" and continued his own climbing.

Upon reaching the top, he found a heavy growth of scrub-oak woods. At the base of a long log, spongy with decay, he started digging, first with his bare hands and then with a strong section of dried branch. Earthworms were abundant in the rich soil, and he quickly unearthed about thirty of them which he tossed into the can along with some of the dirt.

The crossbreed had quickly lost interest in the boy's digging and was now nosing about in a cluster of fallen branches. Unexpectedly a cottontail rabbit sprang out and plunged away with the crossbreed in immediate pursuit. The rabbit was a wise old doe who knew all the tricks and she eluded her pursuer handily, dodging through piles of brush and along a maze of intersecting trails in the deep grasses and finally slipping through the small gap of a hog-wire fence. The young cat gave up the chase and once again began sniffing around through the brushpiles.

With his nose he overturned a large piece of bark and then became extremely busy as at least four or five mice scattered in all directions. He managed to catch and kill two of them, and by the time he had finished eating them, Todd was through with his digging and was calling Yowler to start back down to the boat. In less than five minutes they were once again moving out into the swifter current of the Mississippi.

Todd rigged up a new hook on his line, baited it appealingly with a very wriggly worm and cast it out.

But strangely, now that he had good bait, he got no bites. After a while he became tired of simply sitting there holding the rod, and so he lay on his back on the seat and placed the handle of the rod under him so a fish would not pull it in if one bit. Then he put his canvas tackle bag under his neck and his hands behind his head comfortably and closed his eyes.

The sun was warm on him, and he slept soundly. Late in the afternoon, when it began to cool somewhat, he awoke as a strong tugging came on the line still trailing in the water below. The crossbreed, himself asleep on the front seat, heard the boy stir. He opened his eyes and his tail twitched a time or two.

Todd jerked on the rod instinctively and at once was fighting a fairly good-sized fish. Remembering only too well his previous loss, he took his time with this fish and in a few minutes had landed a largemouth bass just under two pounds. He grinned at the crossbreed, pleased with having reinstated himself as an angler.

In the next quarter hour he caught two more fish, both of them small bluegills, and these he tossed in the bottom of the boat along with the bass, not bothering to put them on the stringer. In the distance ahead of them, a long, narrow island, studded with trees, projected from the center of the river. The sun was already setting, and so Todd reeled in his line, laid his rod on the floor and took up the oars again.

"Guess that'll be as good a place as any to make our first overnight stop, Yowler," he said. "Prob'ly get a little cool. Wish we had a blanket or something. Oh well, a good fire'll keep us warm tonight." He patted the canvas bag in which he kept his matches.

With the aid of the strong current they reached the island quickly. Todd rowed them toward where a long-toppled tree lay in the water, its roots still high on the dry bank and the trunk projecting down into the water and out of sight. He tossed the oars into the bottom of the boat, picked up his canvas tackle bag by its strap and stepped up to the prow of the boat as it coasted the last few feet.

The crossbreed stepped back in the bottom of the boat out of the boy's way and a few feet behind. Todd quickly wrapped the short rope around a branch stub sticking up from the trunk just above where it entered the water.

Todd stepped out onto the broad slanting trunk with one foot, found it firm beneath his weight and drew out the other foot. In doing so, his toe caught the top of the stub. He was thrown off balance and hung there precariously for a moment; then the stub snapped at the base. He flung his arms wildly and the canvas tackle bag sailed through the air and thudded onto the shore. But Todd himself plummeted into the water with a sharp cry and then came up gasping and sputtering.

The water was quite deep here, well over his head, and when his flailing grasp brushed the trunk of the tree, he caught it and pulled himself to it. A low, frightened yowl touched his ears. He turned his head and was dismayed to see the boat already a dozen feet away and, caught by the current, picking up speed as it drifted farther from shore.

Todd could swim if need be, but he was by no means a good swimmer, and though he briefly considered striking out after the boat, he was afraid he would not be able to catch it and would therefore drown. The crossbreed was standing on the prow seat staring bewilderedly around him, and now the urgent voice of the boy reached him.

"Jump, Yowler, jump! Hurry, you can make it. Jump!"

The crossbreed braced his forefeet on the gunwale and crouched as if to leap, but then, as if he, too, thought better of it, drew back and stood upright on the seat again. The yowl that left him now was a disconsolate one, long and wavering.

The gap separating them widened rapidly as the full force of the current swept the boat away. Behind him, Todd had climbed up onto the leaning trunk and crouched there miserably. He was sobbing and his voice was almost unintelligible as he continued screaming at the crossbreed to jump. Finally, even this degenerated into a wailing cry that faded away. For as long as the young animal could see him in the gathering dusk, Todd remained perched where he was; and then he was out of sight.

For the second time in his short life, after more than ten weeks with the boy, the crossbreed was once again alone and adrift on North America's mightiest river.

The darkness came quickly, and the details of the shoreline faded from view. As if suddenly fearful of standing upright on the seat like this, the young crossbreed got down into the bottom of the boat. The scent of the three fish lying there smote his nostrils and reminded him that he was quite hungry; the frog and two mice, caught earlier in the day, had long since been digested.

He dragged the large bass out from under the seat and began eating it. Its flesh was firm and white and very tasty, and he ate until he could hold no more. When he finished, his stomach was well distended and there was very little of the bass left—the head, tail and neatly cleaned spine.

Satisfied, he moved to the stern of the boat where he relieved himself and then, appearing not at all concerned about his predicament, curled up beneath the middle seat and immediately went to sleep. Throughout the night the boat drifted along smoothly and without incident.

Several times during the long night the young crossbreed awakened and raised his head to listen. Once he got to his feet and stood staring silently upward as he drifted beneath a large bridge spanning the river far above him. He heard faintly a car honk its horn. Another time, not more than forty yards to one side of him, a huge boat chugged by, heading upstream, and he watched it curiously until its lights disappeared behind him. The wake it left was not strong at all by the time it reached the little boat, and there was only a momentary, light rocking motion.

Shortly after dawn he awoke again and stretched

grandly, first arching his back high and then stretching out his forepaws and bending low. He took a few short steps and in turn stretched each hind leg far out in back of him and then yawned widely. The sky was heavily overcast, and there was the smell of approaching rain. Hardly a breath of air was stirring, but from the west came a deep rumbling of distant thunder.

He relieved himself again close to the same spot he had used before and then at once centered his attention on the two remaining fish. He ate heads and all of these two, leaving behind only a few bony plates and the spines. He sniffed halfheartedly at the remains of the bigger fish, but finally turned away and hopped nimbly to the middle seat. Here he lay with his feet beneath him, dozing.

About an hour later a heavy gust of wind rippled the water with surprising suddenness, half turning the boat around. The young crossbreed raised his head and looked around him with a trace of nervousness. Just over the bluffs lining the western shore of the river there was a heavy blanket of very dark blue-gray clouds.

A brilliant jagged streak of lightning crashed out of the cloud bank and lanced down to the bluffs, followed almost instantly by a teeth-rattling crash of thunder. Instantly the young crossbreed was off the seat and crouched beneath it, trembling. A deep, frightened moaning whined from him, and now, as the wind struck with a fury, followed moments later by pelting rain and more thunder and lightning, he dug his claws into the bottom of the boat and held on tightly.

The worst of the electrical part of the storm passed in fifteen or twenty minutes, but the heavy rains persisted for more than two hours. When the rain had tapered off to a light drizzle, more than three inches of water covered the bottom of the boat, and the misery of the young crossbreed increased. His trembling was now more from the cold and wetness than from actual fear and he had little choice of position; beneath the seat he was protected from the drizzle and the occasional gusts of wind which still made the river choppy, but under the protection of the seat he was forced to crouch in cold water, and this was even more uncomfortable.

He climbed back onto the prow seat. It was narrow and trapezoidal, and when he curled up on it, his rear quarters were pressing against one side of the boat and his head and shoulders against the other. The very solidness of this position was a comfort to him and it was in this attitude that he remained for the rest of the day and all through the night.

X

The skies were still heavily overcast in the first light of morning and they changed very little throughout the day. The rain, at least, ceased falling shortly after dawn, and the day warmed considerably; but the wind remained strong in its occasional gusts, and the water was choppy and quite roily.

There was little boat traffic on the river this day, and those boatmen who did note the little drifting craft did not pay much attention to it. Had the boat been in better shape, perhaps someone might have investigated; but since it was a decrepit craft at best, and since it was not too infrequent an occurrence for small boats to break their moorings and drift downstream, particularly after a storm, no one much cared.

Time after time the boat drifted to within forty or fifty feet of one shore or another, especially at the places where great curves in the river swung the current shoreward. Twice the drifting boat came quite close to islands. At such times the young crossbreed had been tempted to jump and swim for land, but his natural aversion to water and the fact that he'd already spent a miserably wet night stayed him.

Although the boat frequently swung with the current

and once even made a complete half-turn, mostly it just drifted sideways to the current. Several times during the day it rained again, though never very hard or for very long, and, finally, a half hour before sunset, the clouds broke and the sun appeared for the first time. The air remained balmy, and gradually the young crossbreed lost his soggy look and commenced cleaning himself.

He was extremely hungry, but the remains of the three fish lay in the bottom of the boat, under water made muddy by the overturned can of worms and dirt. His distaste for stepping into the water to get the miserable remains overruled his hunger for the moment. He sat upright on the front seat, idly watching the shore-lines as the current swept him past, and at length, when it became dark once more, he resumed his tightly curled position on the prow seat.

Hunger awoke him off and on during the first part of the night, and if he had had room to do so, he would undoubtedly have paced back and forth. Unable to do this, he contented himself with changing his position frequently, sometimes standing with both front feet on the prow, other times turning nervously in all but tail-catching circles on the limited space of the front seat.

It was during one of those times when he stood with his feet on the prow that he saw lights far downstream. There had been many lights before, from towns, scattered houses and occasionally from autos on highways running parallel with the river, but he seemed to be drawing closer to these new lights with abnormal speed. And then, faintly at first but with increasing tempo, came the dull, throbbing sound of a powerful engine.

The throbbing quickly grew louder, and he could also hear faintly and from some distance ahead, the heavy gurgling of disturbed water. Attentive, though not really alarmed, the young crossbreed stepped back from the prow and stood erect on the front seat. What he saw in the light of the newly risen moon caused him to stiffen with sudden fear—the bulk of a massive craft bearing down on him.

It was an enormous steel barge, incredibly wide,

easily twice as long as its width and many thousands of tons in weight. It sat relatively low in the water, and now, as it drew even closer, the rush of the water smashing against its blunt forward plates rose in volume until it sounded like the crashing of a waterfall. It was immediately apparent that the tiny rowboat, while not directly in the path of this dreadful juggernaut, could not possibly avoid being struck.

The outer corner of the barge caught the rowboat solidly in its center with a great thudding crash, punctuated by the splintering of wood, as the old boat literally disintegrated. The fact that the engines maintained their steady throbbing indicated that the personnel aboard were not even aware that the small craft had been struck.

The bow seat of the rowboat burst outward, catapulting the young crossbreed twenty feet or more through the air. The instant he hit the water, the great surging bow wave of the barge closed over him. He was rolled over under the water for some distance and struggled wildly to regain the surface. He was so badly buffeted by the turbulent water that he could not even find the surface. The swirling eddies spun him in brief circles, and then his head abruptly broke into fresh air and he gasped and sputtered.

Less than five yards from him, the side of the great barge was still hissing past and the roar of the engines was even louder. Instinctively he swam away from it. It was well that he did; as the brightly lighted wheelhouse at the stern of the vessel passed by, there was a heavy reverse current which swept him back into the course over which the boat had just traversed.

Though the danger of that big craft was gone, the young crossbreed was by no means out of his predicament. The little rowboat had been close to midstream at the time of the collision, and now, in the strongest of the current, he was swept rapidly along. Holding his head high, he struck out cross-current, but his progress was slow and taxed his strength severely.

He found that he could maintain himself afloat with little effort at short intervals, and so he alternated swimming vigorously and then resting on the surface while the current pulled him relentlessly downstream. He grew progressively weaker and floated more often than previously; but now that he was trying to rest his legs more as he floated, some of the buoyancy seemed to leave him, and every now and again his head would submerge. Each time he surfaced again, sputtering and hacking. It was evident he could not much longer keep himself from drowning. He so badly lost his sense of direction that several times he found himself swimming the wrong way and doggedly turned back so that the current was once again hitting his right side.

Unexpectedly he was thrown against something wooden and solid. His claws dug in desperately while the current continued to pull at him as if determined to rip him free and reclaim him for a watery end. For a long time he held on, gradually and most carefully moving around until he was on the downcurrent side of the heavy wooden post and the buffeting of the current was not so strong against him.

After resting awhile, the young crossbreed recovered himself enough to see that above him, some ten or twelve feet, was a wooden platform and that projecting from the water around him were other pilings reaching upward to this platform and even extending above it. He had brushed up against a large and well-built pier.

Tentatively he disengaged the claws on one of his front feet, raised the foot several inches higher and dug them in again. Repeating the process with his other front foot and then with his hind feet, he slowly began climbing the piling. Once, when a splinter of wood tore out under his weight when he was about six feet off the water, he very nearly fell backwards.

It took him almost half an hour to reach the top and drag himself onto the level platform of the pier. Here he lay wholly without motion, except for the heaving of his sides, for well over an hour more, resting the strained muscles and regaining his strength. At last, very wearily, he got to his feet and walked shoreward down the length of the long structure.

At the shore end, the pier became an extensive flight of stairs and a long smooth ramp leading upward to a rusting, tin-sided building beside which rested a string of railroad boxcars on a spur line. While he was averse to approaching the building too closely, short of climbing back down one of the support posts, there was no way for him to get to the ground. So he made his way slowly and cautiously up the steps.

A whole series of round, binlike buildings stretched out at the top of the bluff behind the principal tin structure, and almost at once upon reaching the top of the stairs the cat caught the scent of prey. As if by magic, much of his weariness seemed to fall away, and he became keenly alert, his ears drawn back and his body in a half-crouch. Along the platform beside the building—which was more or less a continuation of the pier's structure—he moved rapidly in that peculiar flowing manner. He stayed very close to the wall of the building until he came to the corner, and there he stopped and peered cautiously around it.

The wooden platform followed that side of the building as well, and another string of boxcars was close to the edge of it. Between the cars and the building, no more than twenty feet from the young crossbreed, five rats were clustered about a paper bag. They were energetically and noisily engaged in tearing the paper away to get at two stale doughnuts apparently discarded or forgotten by some worker.

For a long moment the young crossbreed studied them, his tail twitching nervously. He was inclined to dash upon them at once, but, as if thinking better of it, instead he eased his body around the corner, virtually sliding along close to the building's base. Had he dashed at them from such a distance, they would have been alerted at once and very likely escaped; but his stealthy approach remained unnoticed by them until he had very neatly cut that distance by two-thirds.

Suddenly one of the rats squealed piercingly, and instantly there was a confused scurrying as they scattered. The pair closest to the building ran for the bottom of a wide loading door where there was a gap so narrow that they had to press themselves almost flat to squeeze under. Another raced off along the platform at top speed, while the pair on the side away from the building swiftly jumped the small gap into the yawning doorway of a boxcar and vanished into its interior darkness.

The rat which ran down the platform had made a grave mistake, and he compounded the error by abruptly turning back and trying to squeeze under the building door after his two companions. The young crossbreed intercepted him a few inches from the door and felt the bones snap as his teeth closed over the rodent's shoulders and back.

A fearful shriek escaped the rat as it died, and almost before the muscles had stopped their final twitching the young crossbreed was devouring him. He ate with considerable haste, ripping chunks of the flesh away and gulping them down. In a short while he had finished it and once again took up the hunt.

The platform followed the entire perimeter of the building, and he padded around the second corner and was approaching the third when once again he went into his sinuous crouch. He poked his head around the corner just enough to see. Immediately he drew back. A solitary rat was rapidly coming toward this corner from the other direction, running along close to the building with a queer, hopping shuffle.

It was doubtful that this rat even suspected he might be in danger, for his speed hardly slackened as he came to the corner and turned it. In that same instant the crossbreed had him, and this time there wasn't even the opportunity for a death cry. Again the cat fed heartily from the flesh of his prey, though this time he did not attack the meat with that overhungry frenzy he had evinced with the first.

When the rat was all gone, the young crossbreed

remained where he was. Obviously feeling much better now, he cleansed himself thoroughly. It took him the better part of an hour to complete his toilet, and when he began walking again, he stepped along almost jauntily, his head held high and ears alertly lifted, his eyes bright and clear. It was amazing how much better he felt. The food had done wonders for him, and though he was still hungry enough to eat another rat if he could catch one, the ravening pangs that had been wracking him were now gone.

He continued his circuit around the building and soon came back to the place where he had initially encountered the five rats. The deck was deserted except for the food bag, and he trotted to it and sniffed at the partially nibbled and dried-out doughnuts. They did not appeal to him, and he backed away from the bag. Then, remembering the pair of rats that had vanished into the dark cavern of the boxcar, he poised briefly on the edge of the platform and craned his neck in order to look inside. Dimly he could see a pile of slatted pieces of wood and heavy paper in a jumble, intermingled with a cluster of straw. This same straw material was scattered over most of the floor of the car.

He hopped nimbly across the gap and made a circuit of the boxcar's interior. Near the pile of materials he was sure he detected scent from the rats, but he made no effort to ferret them out. Instead, he took a position against the near wall of the car, settled himself comfortably in the straw and within moments had fallen into a deep slumber He was extremely tired and he slept very well.

The interior of the car was plainly visible in the morning light when he was awakened by the sound of a man's voice. At once he was on his feet. Clinging close to the side of the car, he moved to the doorway and poked his head out, immediately jerking back when he saw a man approaching along the platform.

There was another sound then, a deep, powerful rumble in the direction of the far end of the building, and suddenly there was a heavy crashing sound and the

young crossbreed was knocked off his feet as the whole boxcar lurched sharply. He turned completely over in the straw and, surprised but uninjured, regained his balance and crouched with his feet widespread, lest another jolt knock him over again.

It was well he did so. A moment later, with a second jolt as violent as the first, the boxcar began moving. Outside, the platform was moving by with increasing speed, then trees and brush whizzed past. The rattling and banging changed to the regularly cadenced clicking of the wheels over the track junctions.

Frightened at first by such a dizzying and still increasing speed, yet undoubtedly curious, the young crossbreed approached the open door gradually, almost crawling along on his stomach. He stopped a foot from the door and lay there watching the countryside go by. The wind stirred by the train's passage ruffled his fur pleasantly, and his fear diminished and was replaced by something akin to enjoyment.

He caught a glimpse of the great Mississippi River as the train followed its course downstream for a few miles, but then lost sight of it as the rails angled away to assume a more southwesterly course. In a little while the train was speeding through long, unbroken stretches of scrub-oak woods and past occasional highway crossings where warning bells clanged sharply for an instant and then were lost in the distance behind.

For most of the day he lay there with his forepaws outstretched, reminiscent of a little lion surveying his realm through placid eyes. Now and then he arose and prowled through the car. On one such occasion he selected a corner farthest from the door in which to paw an opening in the straw, relieve himself and then cover his droppings.

Always, however, he seemed drawn back to the doorway to continue his hypnotic staring at the unraveling countryside. Twice during the day the car stopped —once very briefly and again for an hour or more—but both times the voices of men nearby caused him to withdraw to a dim corner of the car and crouch deeply in the straw, rather than make any attempt to jump out.

For a cat only half a year old and still not much advanced beyond kittenhood, the young crossbreed had already traveled a considerable distance from his birthplace and, most certainly, by some rather spectacular means. As dusk was falling, the train picked up speed again, and now, with the miles spinning off regularly behind him, it was apparent that the crossbreed's odyssey had only begun.

XI

After that first day, his initial interest in the impromptu train ride wore off, degenerating first to boredom and then to a marked restlessness. By the end of his fourth day in the boxcar, the journey had become almost intolerable, decidedly worsened by hunger and thirst.

On the second day, as the train snaked through east-central Missouri, one of the pair of rats in the car made the fatal mistake of showing himself too boldly. With consummate skill the crossbreed had pounced upon him after a short, stealthy stalk. He ate him as neatly as the train ate up the miles. The second rat, however, aware of its danger and the fate of its companion, remained well hidden under the wood, paper and straw debris, and even though the young crossbreed began determinedly tearing at the pile on the evening of the third day, the rodent managed to elude him.

The farther south this slow freight train had rolled, the warmer the weather had become, and the more humid. For the past six or seven hours the train had clattered leisurely through a peculiarly alien countryside, a region in which great gnarled oaks and towering cypress, holly and tupelo trees were enshrouded with long flowing strands of Spanish moss. They passed innumerable lakes and ponds and sluggish river systems, collectively called bayous in this country, and in and around them there was an incredible abundance of wildlife. Impressive flocks of herons and egrets and ibises filled the air, and lone birds stood silently on their polelike legs in knee-deep water or perched in solitude on stumps or low branches or cypress knees close to the water.

Numerous times over the past days and several times during the past two hours the train had slowed considerably and moved along at a speed not much greater than the crossbreed might have run. At such times the crossbreed had balanced precariously on the edge of the doorway, preparatory to leaping out, yet still hesitant to do so. Each time the train had ultimately picked up more speed again, and he had resumed his restless vigil.

At last, on the fifth morning, the train entered a large switchyard at the outskirts of the Louisiana city of Alexandria and there it came to a jolting halt. As at previous stops, the sounds of men talking and moving about reached him, and the young crossbreed shrank away from the doorway and crouched against the far wall. On this occasion, however, a man poked his head in the doorway, startling him into a frightened bound to the rear corner of the car, and an exclamation broke from the man. At once he clambered up into the car and began advancing on the animal, brandishing in his hand a strong stick about four feet in length.

As he came closer, the young cat moved to avoid him, but anticipating just such a move, the man sidestepped and poked the stick at him and forced him back into the corner. A low, warning growl rolled from the crossbreed's throat, and his back hunched. His hackles raised, and his tufted ears flattened against his skull. The sharp white teeth showed plainly as he snarled, and the man, now becoming more cautious, maintained a respectful distance, holding the stick in a half-raised position from which he could use it either for striking or poking with equal facility.

The stick was suddenly thrust at him, and though the young crossbreed dodged to one side, it punched his ribs painfully and nearly turned him over. The cat's growl of fear and warning turned now to one of combined pain and rage. As the stick poked at him again, he deftly slapped it to one side with a forepaw and instantly charged this formidable enemy.

A startled oath escaped the man, and though he swung the club viciously now, he missed. The next instant the crossbreed had flung himself into the man's legs, clinging with his foreclaws to his thigh while his hind legs pumped piston-like and the fierce rear claws ripped at the man's shin, shredding the cloth and digging deep gouges in his flesh. At the same moment, the strong teeth sank even more deeply into the thick muscles just above the knee.

The man screamed in pain and fear and swung his club again. This time he caught the crossbreed across the hind haunch with a blow that knocked the animal several feet through the air. The cat was on his feet and charging back to the attack the instant he hit, and now the tables were turned; it was the man who was backed into the corner, waving his stick menacingly before him and screeching at the top of his lungs.

"Charlie! *Charlie!* Help me!"

From some distance away outside came another man's voice. His feet crunched rapidly on the coarse gravel as he ran toward them. Eyes bugged with fear and his right leg now bleeding profusely, the club-wielder screamed again.

"Your gun, Charlie! Hurry, use your gun! Shoot him! This thing's trying to kill me!"

The other man appeared at the doorway, sized up the situation in an instant and tugged at the snap of his holster flap. Though he couldn't know what was coming, the young crossbreed did know again it was he who was at a disadvantage and he lost no time in acting. He spun about and, even as the outside man was drawing the heavy revolver from its holster, he bounded over his head.

The man who was called Charlie ducked fearfully and then, while still crouched, leveled his handgun at the young crossbreed. The animal was already racing away at top speed, parallel to the train, when the first shot came. An explosion of pain caused him to stagger as the gun banged and the slug tore a hot shallow trench across his right hip.

Instantly the crossbreed dodged, plunging under the cars and out the other side. Another shot spanged viciously off a wheel close to him and he dodged again, ran under another string of slowly moving boxcars and then once again sped pellmell down the trackbed.

No further shots came, but he maintained his galloping speed, heading toward a dense grove of moss-bedecked trees in the distance at the far end of this shunting yard. He was breathing raggedly from his efforts when he reached them, but still he did not pause. Not until he had plunged through a quarter mile or more of the heavy underbrush did he slow down and continue his passage at an easier pace.

In another ten minutes he came to a gigantic live oak tree lying on the ground, its bole shattered either from a lightning bolt or broken as the result of a strong wind, and its trunk hollow for twenty feet or more. He sniffed at the entrance curiously and, detecting nothing to alarm him, stepped into the hollow and followed it to where it split into two smaller hollows following main branches. Here, his sides still heaving, he lay down and rested for a long while, eventually falling asleep.

It was late afternoon when he awakened, and an involuntary little sound of pain escaped him. His side, where the yardman's stick had poked him, was tender and sore, and the bullet crease on his hip had crusted and hurt even worse, especially when he moved and caused the wound to split. For the next hour he licked it thoroughly and much relieved its aching. The bullet had broken the skin in a swath perhaps two inches long, but had only seared the muscle tissue.

With the coming of early dusk his hunger returned in an overpowering wave, and he left the haven of the

hollow tree trunk, limping only a little. A melange of
new and exciting aromas filled the air—scents from
flowers and plants, swamps and wild creatures of the
Louisiana bayou country with which he was wholly
unfamiliar. Strange air plants with foliage similar to
small pineapples grew profusely from the branches and
crotches of living trees, and the long streamers of Spanish moss draped over gnarled limbs—limbs which were
further punctuated here and there with large clumps of
ball moss.

The air was heavy and vibrant with life. Egrets and
ibises returning to their roosts for the night flashed
whitely above the trees, and occasional late-flying
pileated woodpeckers, larger than crows, bounced
across dusky clearings and over expansive bayous with
a queer, jerky flight.

From far off came the stirring, chattering cry of a
raccoon, and from closer at hand something large and
heavy and peculiarly ominous swirled the dark waters
with a deep gurgling sound. The evening's first call of a
screech owl, muted and pleasant, rose quaveringly from
a dense thicket across the closest bayou, repeating itself
three times before lapsing into silence.

The nose of the young crossbreed wrinkled as he
raised his head to catch and endeavor to identify the
variety of scents. At each new sound his ears twitched
and turned with the same effort. Surprisingly, as he
walked now toward the nearest bayou, keenly alert to
everything around him, he showed little effect from the
injuries he had suffered in the switching yard.

For a long while he stood on the bank of the bayou
and sniffed suspiciously at the strangely dark water. He
had never seen or smelled any water quite like it before. Though it was a very deep brown—stained so by
the tannin from various trees and plants growing from
or fallen into the bayou and decaying—it was not
murky at all, but rather a clear brown with the
transparent quality of amber, and its aroma was not at
all unpleasant to him. He lowered his head and lapped,

hesitantly at first, but then more eagerly. He was very thirsty.

Almost immediately, as he began moving along the bank, there was a flurry of activity as several pickerel frogs and quite a large bullfrog leaped away and plunged into the bayou. At once his hunting instinct took over and he crept along the bank more carefully. Other frogs continued to leap away, but without much difficulty he caught five in succession and gulped them down.

Emboldened by his success and the fact that he was apparently free of attack from men here, he began to pay more attention to his hunting than to his watchfulness for danger. When he came to a point where the bayou narrowed to no more than a dozen feet, he could see in the last dim traces of daylight a half-submerged log projecting out of the water and spanning most of this distance. He leaped nimbly onto it and began to cross.

When he was halfway to the other shore, the log lurched suddenly, and there came a terrifying hissing roar. A tremendous, many-toothed set of gaping jaws rose from the end toward which he was moving and jerked sharply toward him. At the same time the long, craggy tail, stretched out behind, swung forward in a powerful slashing arc.

The young crossbreed dug in his claws and held on, his reaction more instinctive than reasoned. Once again the tail of the nine-foot alligator slashed forward, smacking the water with a great splash, while the vicious head snapped to the side again. Still the cat held his grip, but not for long.

In a savage twisting maneuver, the alligator twice spun his entire body over in the water to dislodge his rider. As soon as his own body was submerged, the crossbreed loosed his grip and struck out frantically for the shore. The alligator stopped rolling and surfaced and, most fortunately for his intended prey, came up directly beneath him.

The young crossbreed found a precarious purchase on the deeply ridged back and raced along it. His feet bunched for an instant on the back of the alligator's head just behind the great protuberant eyes and, even as the reptile simultaneously raised and swung his head, the crossbreed leaped as far as he could. His front legs caught the spongy shoreline and dug in. Although the alligator surged immediately to follow up his attack, the cat was quicker. He pulled himself out of the water and plunged away through the dense ground cover of the dark swampland.

Behind him, the crossbreed could still hear the alligator thrashing about in the water, but the sound quickly died away as he continued to run. He galloped at top speed for several hundred yards before realizing that he was not being pursued.

It had been an extremely close call, and he had learned a good lesson from it. There was obviously dangers to himself here with which he was unfamiliar. Until he came to know this country and its inhabitants better, it would behoove him to proceed with considerable care. Most certainly he would not again blithely leap onto a partially submerged log without first making very sure that it was, indeed, a log.

So began the crossbreed's residence in a strange new world.

XII

In the eighteen months since his arrival in the bayou country, the crossbreed had changed considerably. By no stretch of the imagination could he any longer be considered a kitten or, for that matter, even a young cat. He had adapted well to his change of habitat and would undoubtedly have lived a full and pleasant life here if it hadn't been for the persistent, gnawing restlessness within him.

Ever since reaching this country, he had periodically engaged in a strange ritual: he would stand quietly for long minutes with his head cocked to the north, listening intently, staring fixedly, deeply sniffing the air, yet not for any of the sounds or sights or odors of the country immediately around him. It was as if he yearned for something he could not quite comprehend, and it built within him a prevailing uneasiness bordering on discontent.

Almost two years old now, he stood thirteen inches high at the shoulder, and from the end of his nose to the tip of his stubby tail he was fully thirty-two inches long. He weighed twenty-eight pounds, and it seemed likely that he would gain considerably more weight than that, for he was rather lean and lithe and very tightly muscled.

Physically, his bobcat heritage was markedly evident; only the markings on his fur closely resembled those of the feral cat that had borne him. Though his clean and luxuriant fur had the basic undercoloring of tawny brown-gray like that of any bobcat, his stripings of deep gray-black were decidedly those of his mother. His clear, intelligent eyes remained an odd blend of colors: basically yellowish-orange and yet always with that peculiar gray-green cast to them.

He was now an extremely agile and self-confident creature, possessing the knack of quickly adapting to whatever situation he encountered, of quickly learning from the few errors he made and not repeating them. He seemed to recognize the fact that there were few creatures in this country he had cause to fear, and many with every reason for fearing him. He was an expert, tenacious and merciless hunter, and he carried himself proudly, with something of the regality so often inherent in members of the cat family.

The bayou country had undoubtedly proved beneficial to him over these many months, and he had learned well the lessons for survival in it: how to hunt the prey which sustained him and yet avoid those creatures which were dangerous to him. Rarely, if ever, did he not eat well.

Through that first autumn and winter he had fed on a great variety of creatures—birds, reptiles, amphibians and mammals. Occasionally he even caught and devoured many of the larger insects—giant grasshoppers and crickets and huge cinnamon-colored roaches. As time passed, he settled on marsh rabbits, deer mice and voles as the mainstay of his diet, though sometimes other rodents also fell prey to him, including muskrats and woodchucks, pack rats and Norway rats.

Birds were abundant; a few species nesting on the ground but most on low branches. The nests of the snakebirds and the waders—herons, egrets and ibises—

were flimsy, built of crudely interwoven twigs to form somewhat concave platforms. The fledglings in them were easy to reach, but after a few encounters with irate parent birds, he left them alone unless absolutely nothing else was available.

Although occasionally he still ate frogs and, even more frequently, small snakes, he had a distinct preference for the warm-blooded meat of mammals, especially rodents. Besides, most of the frogs and some of the snakes buried themselves under mud or leaves or in decomposing logs for most of the cooler period from mid-December through mid-March.

In feeding upon rodents, particularly mice, the crossbreed encountered some pretty stiff competition. Among the predators who actively sought them were gray foxes and minks, skunks and raccoons and occasional otters, hawks and owls, great blue herons, many kinds of snakes, armadillos and weasels. None of these creatures—with the exception of a couple of the snakes —posed any real physical threat to the crossbreed and usually they would, depending upon the species, beat a hasty or dignified retreat at his approach.

Only the skunk would hold his ground and, after his first encounter with one, it was the crossbreed who kept a respectful distance. Two species of skunk lived here: the common striped skunk and the little spotted skunk, which was less than half the size of the former. Both had very powerful spray ducts located directly beneath the tail and both could shoot their nauseous, oily liquid accurately for a distance of ten feet or more.

The crossbreed met his first skunk within a month of his arrival in the bayou country, during the period when he was still learning about the country and its inhabitants. Though the spray from the little spotted skunk did not strike his eyes as it was meant to, it did spatter his chest fur, forelegs and one side. So sickening was the stench that he had instantly lost all desire but to rid himself of it—and that took some doing. For many weeks afterward, the scent still clinging to his fur continued to plague and irritate him. Since then he maintained his distance from these black-and-white mammals possessing so powerful a weapon.

There were really only three wild creatures in this country dangerous to the crossbreed, and two of them were, for the most part, easily avoided: the alligator and the cottonmouth moccasin. Both species preferred to stay in or near the bayou waters. The third, however, was a constant threat against which he remained alert: the canebrake rattlesnake, southern subspecies of the vile-tempered and always dangerous timber rattler. A peculiarly mottled, yellowish snake, it grew as thick as a man's arm and to a length of seventy inches; its hollow fangs, filled with deadly venom, could cause another animal's death in a very short time.

It was during that initial February after his arrival that the crossbreed inadvertently had a close call with just such a serpent. Normally he sensed the presence of one of these pit vipers long before he came within the snake's striking range and instinctively he detoured. But on this occasion his attention had been centered on a large bobcat, and not until too late did he realize the danger.

Although bobcats were not numerous in this bayou country, and those that were here ranged widely, nevertheless he did cross the paths of a few. Mostly he fled when this happened, since at that time they were larger and more formidable than he. But then in mid-February, when he was nearly a year old, as he had stood facing to the north again, listening, looking, sniffing and mostly lost to the habitat in which he was actually standing, an impelling aroma abruptly shook him out of his reverie. Instinctively he began following it to its source and within fifteen minutes he encountered a delicate, yearling, female bobcat.

She flattened her ears and snarled as he approached, but now something stirred in him which negated any idea he may have had of turning tail. He matched her low, whining growl with one of his own, and sinking into a half-crouch, began circling her in the clearing.

She turned as he circled, always facing him, and though the growl continued to roll from her, it was more of an invitation than a warning to the ears of the crossbreed.

He sprang toward her suddenly and she rolled over onto her back and grappled with him, her hind claws raking his underside shallowly and her teeth biting him hard enough to hurt sharply, but not injure. Back and forth they thrashed across the clearing before she broke away and ran swiftly.

Without hesitation he followed closely on her heels, through woods, along fallen tree trunks, up into the low crotches of huge live oaks and black willows, across sandy bars overgrown with low saw grass. Three times he overtook her and three times they clinched, though each time her growls were less threatening, her bites and clawings less painful.

At last she sank to the earth in a small sandy clearing, and her voice was now more of a compelling, whining song than a growl. She was willing to accept him as mate, and the crossbreed understood this and his own excitement became subtly subdued.

Not for long, however.

A twig snapped to one side of them, and a deep menacing growl reached both of them. Instantly the crossbreed's ears flattened, and his mouth opened in an answering snarl which was clearly a warning. Partially crouched, he held his ground and watched through slitted eyes the approach of a large battle-scarred male bobcat.

The rival, easily half again the size of the crossbreed, stepped stiff-leggedly out of the underbrush into the clearing, and there could be no doubt he meant to have this young female as his own. His ears, too, were tight against his head and his hackles were raised from nape to tail. He did not even glance at the female, knowing she would remain, but rather kept his eyes locked upon the crossbreed, and again the battle cry rumbled in his throat.

Not in the least perturbed, the female watched the two males alertly. The crossbreed had all but won her, yet not quite, and should this larger male defeat him, which seemed altogether probable, she would undoubtedly accept the victor as mate—provided he could win her as the crossbreed had.

Just as obviously, the crossbreed considered that he had irrevocably won her already, and even though his heart was hammering heavily within him and a current of fear caused him to tremble slightly, he held his ground. And when the bigger cat sprang to the attack, he leaped to meet him and they joined in a fierce and desperate combat.

Rarely in such battles as this were either of the combatants slain, but the loser was more often than not in sad condition at the conclusion; he must either flee or else expose his underside and whine his surrender. Both alternatives were highly distasteful and spiritually crushing to the loser.

From the onset in this fight, however, it was evident that the crossbreed would have little chance against the larger cat. He fought well and managed to add several new claw and tooth wounds to the numerous scars borne by the older cat, but for every mark he gave his opponent, he received more than equal measure in return.

Out of the clearing they rolled and into the denser growth, and still they fought and tore savagely at one another. At one point they broke apart for an instant, and the crossbreed, courage badly faltering, began to race away. In a dozen yards the older male overtook him and once again they clinched in furious battle.

Intent upon their own conflict, they neither heard nor saw the thick-bodied canebrake rattler coiled beside a moss-encrusted log. Tightly bunched, the snake held its head a half foot off the ground and its tail vibrated in a loud warning buzz. The combatants suddenly rolled toward it, and the large reptile struck.

By the narrowest of margins the great fangs missed the upper foreleg of the crossbreed and instead plunged deeply into the side of the bobcat's neck. At once the snake disengaged and recoiled, but the two cats rolled back in the other direction, still locked together.

In moments a fearful screech erupted from the big male. He released his hold on the crossbreed and jumped back crazily, eyes rolling wildly. He half fell, regained his feet and moved as if to clinch again with the crossbreed. Then his legs collapsed and he fell to his side on the ground, his body shaking violently. He kicked frantically and his mouth opened and closed rapidly, though no further sound escaped his throat. Once he almost succeeded in regaining his feet, but then his back arched so tightly in the wrong direction and his legs stuck out from his body so stiffly that it actually seemed the straining muscles would cause his bones to break. For perhaps fifteen or twenty seconds he lay frozen like this, then he relaxed, his eyes half closed, and just that quickly he was dead.

Deeply afraid, the young crossbreed had watched the final contortions of his adversary, observing at the same time that the rattler was still coiled to strike alongside the log. He backed away a few feet more, even though he was well out of range. When the bobcat died, he turned to find the female and discovered her standing only a short distance from him.

She advanced to him now and licked the side of his face. With no further courtship preliminaries and not another glance at the fallen bobcat, they padded off together. They mated at intervals and stayed together, hunting, sleeping and playing for more than a month; but when the female showed no sign of pregnancy at the end of that time, their attitude toward one another cooled. They spent considerably longer periods apart, and then one day, the discontent rising in him again, the crossbreed raised his head to the north and stood motionlessly for several minutes. When abruptly he padded away without a glance at her, the female did not follow him.

The crossbreed did not return.

XIII

His parting from the female bobcat during that first spring in the bayou country had marked the beginning of a rather unusual change in the crossbreed's habits. Previously he had made a large cavity in the bole of a giant American holly tree his permanent den and had ranged in an area of about five miles around it, always returning to it; now, he rarely stayed in one den for any great while.

For a week or two, perhaps even for a month, he would be content in a new den, but then the restlessness would grip him anew and he would give in to the urge which gradually drew him northward. In just over a year he lived in nineteen different locations, each site anywhere from two to ten miles north of the previous one.

Now, in his second spring in the south, he found himself on the northernmost fringe of the bayou country where the low swampy areas and multitude of bayous gave way to a drier and higher habitat; where the tupelo and sweet gum, cypress and black willow gave way to hickory and white oak, elm, beechnut and yellow pine. It was here that he met, wooed and won another small female bobcat, this time unrivaled in his advances.

While she was older, she was not quite so large as his first mate. Though at first she had fended off his advances with considerable vigor, she had quickly given in to him and they had mated and established a den deep within a rocky cleft which jutted from a low hill. She was three, a year older than the crossbreed, and they shared a devotion which, though deep, was destined to be brief.

Nothing came of their union. As with the first female, the crossbreed's mate showed no sign of pregnancy; her appetite remained constant rather than increasing, her nipples did not engorge, her abdomen did not begin to swell with new life developing within her. And though neither of them could know it, the truth of the matter was that, as a hybrid, the crossbreed was sterile and would never be capable of siring young.

Undoubtedly he and this mate would have drifted apart, much as had occurred with his first mating, if fate had not intervened. Their present den, overlooking a stream called Bayou Bartholemew, was located perhaps a dozen miles northeast of the Louisiana town of Bastrop. On a warm evening late in March, as they ranged together in a hunting expedition, they neared a macadam highway which ran roughly parallel to the bayou. As usual, the pair kept their distance from it, fearful of the scent of man and machine which prevailed around it.

Due to a shift in the light breeze, they were unaware of the presence of the cottontail rabbit until it suddenly sprang up a dozen yards in front of them and bolted away at great speed. Instantly both cats were in hot pursuit. The female was ten or fifteen feet closer to the rabbit than the crossbreed when it sprinted away, and she not only maintained this gap between herself and her mate, but quickly began closing the gap between herself and the rabbit.

They raced along for fifty yards or more in the

ditch running alongside the highway until the rabbit veered, scooted up the bank to the macadam and began to cross. It was a mistake; the bobcat took the incline faster than the rabbit and pounced on her prey in the middle of the far lane of the pavement.

The crossbreed bounded up the rise only seconds behind them, but they were fortuitous seconds. A car's headlights bore down upon them with terrific speed and, as the crossbreed stopped eight feet off the road on the rim of the shoulder to stare at the oncoming lights, so the female raised her own head to stare, the rabbit clenched in her jaws.

Apparently the driver of the car did not see the animal until too late. Tires squealed as the auto swerved violently to miss her, but she was struck solidly. The heavy thudding sound of this initial impact was followed by two muted bumps as the wheels passed over her. The car swayed precariously for a hundred yards or more until its driver brought it back under control. The brake lights flared momentarily, but then the car continued on its way without stopping.

Petrified, the crossbreed remained rooted on the shoulder for several minutes, until even the sound of the auto was lost to his keen hearing. Then he trotted to where she lay, perhaps thirty feet from where she had been standing when struck. Of the rabbit there was no sign; it had either lodged in the grillwork of the auto or been knocked far into the weeds off the road.

The female bobcat was badly mangled, and there could be no doubt she was dead. A tire had passed over her head, crushing it, and even as the crossbreed bent his head to sniff at her flank, another pair of headlights lighted the early darkness in the distance, approaching from the direction in which the first auto had disappeared.

The crossbreed reacted at once, leaping lightly away off the side of the road toward Bayou Bartholemew. He was thirty yards from the road when the vehicle hissed by, but he neither stopped nor turned. If grief filled him at the loss of his mate, he showed no indication of

it. This was a chapter closed. As if he had been primed
for just such an eventuality, he set off upstream at a
steady mile-eating lope, abandoning, without another
thought, the den he had shared with the female.

Before midnight he had unknowingly crossed the
boundary line separating Louisiana and Arkansas and
continued northward along the western bank of the
meandering bayou. Several times during the night he
paused to catch mice or run down a rabbit when he
encountered them, but for the first time his traveling
was on a truer course and more determined than his
previous rambling movements. Not until the light of
breaking dawn did he secrete himself in a cramped
hollow at the base of an ancient oak and remain there
in deep sleep until evening.

During the next four nights he continued traveling in
this essentially northward line until, just a few miles
south of Dumas, the stream took on a westerly heading
which bothered him. Time after time he approached the
bank of the stream and stared across to the other shore,
perhaps forty feet or more distant. He knew he could
swim it without difficulty, but he hesitated entering it.
More than once his life had hung in jeopardy when he
found himself in the water, and he had no intention of
entering it deliberately so long as he was not forced to
do so.

Nevertheless, as the stream angled even more distinctly to the northwest, he grew increasingly nervous.
And when, just west of a tiny Arkansas hamlet named
Crigler, he encountered a narrow highway bridge, he
discarded his usual caution and trotted across it to the
other side.

Once again, at this point, Bayou Bartholemew was
coming from the north, and he continued following it
along the east bank; but in a few miles it resumed its
northwest origin and it was here that the crossbreed
angled away from it. Even though daybreak was again
streaking the east, he was not particularly fatigued and
so he continued his journey.

The countryside here was substantially more farmed

and populated than he had previously encountered farther to the south, and frequently he made wide detours
to avoid individual farmhouses or small communities.
Nevertheless, he had made a serious mistake by traveling in the daytime. For five minutes as he traversed a
wide pastureland and crossed a major highway bisect-
ing it, a pair of binoculars, three-fourths of a mile
distant, had been trained upon him. The eyes followed
his progress and noted with especial care the point at
which he crossed the road, and then their owner ran
inside a large farmhouse.

Moments later three men poured from the doorway.
One leaped into a pickup truck and started its motor,
another ran to a shed and reappeared with a ten-foot
pole and coil of rope, while the third ran to a
high-fenced kennel yard where half a dozen hounds
bounded about eagerly at the gate. Two of them were
Walker hounds, three others were blue ticks and the
last was a large black-and-tan. All three men carried
guns and the dogs, sensing a hunt forthcoming, bayed
and whined. They knew what was expected of them
and, as soon as their gate was opened, they raced to the
truck and leaped into the open bed of it.

The men followed, quickly raising and securing the
tailgate and then crowding into the cab of the truck. A
moment later the vehicle roared northwest along U.S.
Highway 65 toward Pine Bluff. At the point where the
animal had crossed the road, the truck pulled off onto
the shoulder and came to a quick stop, nearly upsetting
the dogs and causing gravel to shower like hail on the
undercarriage.

Not waiting for the tailgate to be lowered, the dogs
vaulted the side and began snuffling about. The men
piled out, and the dogs ran at once to the spot where
the man who had used the binoculars squatted and
pointed to the ground, calling them.

"Get 'im, Dooley, Ruff, Guber. Bobcat! C'mon,
Deke, get 'im!"

The dogs spread out, their noses close to the ground

and the sound of their eager sniffing loud in the early morning stillness. The man, however, had miscalculated just a trifle, and it was the lone black-and-tan hound circling farther out than the rest who caught the fresh scent twenty yards ahead of where the truck was parked. At once he bayed deeply, and the men spun round.

"Ol' Judd's got 'im," yelled one of them.

The black-and-tan was already a hundred feet away and running at a good clip, his snout still low to the ground. The other five dogs fell in behind at once, and now catching the scent themselves, raised their own voices in a strangely stirring chorus.

"Still heading due north," the driver said. "He'll hit the river purty soon. Five'll getcha ten he heads upstream. Let's go!"

He jumped back into the driver's seat, but the other two climbed into the rear to better hear the baying of the pack. The truck lurched forward and traveled a couple of miles, entered and passed through the tiny village of Moscow and then, a short distance out of town on the opposite side, turned right down a two-rut lane heading toward the Arkansas River about two miles to the north. A fringe of woodland lined the river on both sides for about fifty yards. It was at the edge of this that the rutted trail petered out and the truck stopped. The men strained to hear, cupping their hands behind their ears. Within minutes the melodious baying reached them faintly, and all three grinned.

"Comin' this way sure 'nuff, Dee," one of them said. "Reckon he'll tree?"

"Ought'a," replied the driver. "But don't kill 'im iffen he don't, Slim. He'll tree somewheres. He ain't 'bout to swim the river, an' with Ol' Judd an' the others on his trail that hot, he ain't got no choice but to tree purty quick. 'Member, though, don't shoot if he goes past us. Dead we won't get much for 'im, but I know daggone good'n well Big Art'll give us at least twenny-thirty bucks for 'im live."

At this moment the crossbreed was still over a mile and a half from the men, unaware of their presence and running rapidly in their direction. Though he had been more than a mile from the dogs when they first began barking excitedly in their pen, he had heard them easily. Within his ears were sensitive hairs capable of picking up and identifying minute vibrations, and his long slender whiskers worked in much the same manner. He had not been perturbed by the sounds. Often dogs had barked at a distance, and occasionally he had been chased by one or two, but had eluded them.

He thereupon continued his passage through the meadowland and into some scattered scrub-oak growth at his steady trotting pace. A few minutes later, however, he heard the excited, discovery baying of a hound no more than a half-mile behind him, immediately followed by a chorus of excited howls.

Becoming a little nervous, he had broken into a somewhat faster pace, still heading north toward the dense growth of trees he could see a mile and a half ahead. He was not yet certain that it was on his own trail that the hounds were baying, but within two minutes more he was sure of it, and it was then that he put on a burst of speed.

He was a quarter-mile ahead of the dogs when he found the broad Arkansas River barring his path. Briefly he hesitated and then turned in the more northerly direction—upstream—and continued to run.

Every once in a while he tried some evasive tactic. Once leaping up onto a leaning tree trunk and then springing fully twenty feet away and continuing his run; another time backtracking a score of feet or more and then bounding upward into a tree, following a branch into an adjoining tree and climbing to the ground, there to continue his flight.

The dogs on his trail, especially the one called Ol' Judd, were highly experienced trailers, and the crossbreed's evasive tactics were only momentarily successful. Within minutes the dogs were back on his trail, and now a greater fear began to well in him. After traveling nearly twenty miles the preceding night, he had been running at top speed now for almost four miles and his breathing was becoming ragged, his legs tiring. He might have enough stamina for another three or four miles at this pace, but if he did, he would have little strength left with which to fight if that became necessary. It was time to take to a tree. Let the dogs mill about below him; eventually they would weary of waiting and leave.

He literally ran up the trunk of a massive and rather isolated old oak, and at a point some three-fourths up the height of the tree and perhaps sixty-five feet above the ground, he carefully walked out from the trunk on a sturdy five-inch branch and lay outstretched upon it.

Not five hundred yards ahead of him the three men at the truck waited and watched expectantly. The baying of the dogs came even closer and the driver of the truck—the man named Dee—spat a brown stream of tobacco juice to one side.

"Reckon Ol' Judd's either right on that cat's tail or else the critter's done gone an' treed 'tween us'ns an' them."

Two minutes later the pack was baying "treed," and Dee grinned at his companions. "How's that for figgerin', eh?"

They already had their guns, and so now, snatching up the rope and pole from the back of the truck, the trio ran toward the sound of the baying hounds. They arrived puffing and stationed themselves in a triangle under the big tree, all three of them squinting upward through the branches in an effort to see their quarry. It was the youngest of the three who spotted the crossbreed first. He was a cadaverously thin man of about twenty-six with high cheekbones and an amazingly prominent Adam's apple.

"There! I see 'im!" he yelled, pointing toward the high branch.

The other two ran over to him, followed the line of

his outstretched arm and spied the animal at once. The driver slapped the young man on the shoulder approvingly.

"Good goin', Slim. Reckon you kin get up to 'im 'thout any trouble?"

Slim studied the tree gravely and then nodded. "Reckon so, Dee, iffen you'n Andy gimme a boost to that first big branch there." He looked a little worried and his Adam's apple bobbed. "You reckon I kin do it safe, Dee?"

The driver snorted. "Easier'n wringin' a hen's neck, boy. Sure you kin. Do it jest like you done with that there big ol' boar 'coon las' week. Only let 'im down sooner. 'Member, it don't take long for 'em to choke an' that 'coon was 'bout done in by the time you got 'im down to us."

As they talked, Dee had built a slip noose in one end of the rope, ran the long free end of the line through a large screw eye near the outer end of the pole and then down through a similar eye closer to the butt. This trailing end of the rope, perhaps eighty feet of it, he bunched together and tied to the handle of the pole, then laid it aside.

Together, Dee and Andy made cups of their interlocked hands and lifted Slim to the first large crotch. When he was up and had his balance, Andy passed the roped pole up to him. All the while the dogs continued to dance around excitedly below.

"Tell you one thing sure," Slim grunted as he began his branch-by-branch ascent toward the crossbreed, "that 'cat comes at me an' I'm gonna whomp 'im on the head an' let the dawgs get 'im. I ain't hankerin' to tangle with no wil'cat barehanded, 'specially way up there."

Neither Dee nor Andy replied, and he continued to climb. In a few moments he reached the branch upon which the crossbreed perched. The animal had turned around and was now facing him from less than fifteen feet away. A low, hair-raising growl escaped him, and his snarl, baring strong, sharp canine teeth, was highly disconcerting to Slim The man's Adam's apple bounced vigorously.

Straddling the branch, the young man positioned the noose properly beneath the pole and let the long, loose line drop freely below him Then he stretched the pole out in front of him and began inching away from the trunk. The snarling of the crossbreed grew even louder and more formidable; he backed up until he could go no farther without losing his own grip Under the weight of man and cat, the branch bowed considerably, but it neither cracked nor broke.

By now the loop at the end of the outstretched pole dangled before the crossbreed. He slapped a paw at it and time after time knocked it away; but always it swung back. And then one time, because the branch bounced and he dug in his foreclaws to hang on, he did not bat it aside. The loop passed over his head and instantly drew tight around his neck, and Slim let out a bellow of triumph

Though the crossbreed struggled against it as furiously as he could without falling from the branch, the noose drew tighter. His claws dug even more deeply into the wood to hold on against the inexorable pulling His eyes bulged, and a strangling sound left him In a short while his eyes began to glaze, and at the end of another minute he lost consciousness and toppled He swung pendulously ten feet below his captor.

"That's it, Slim, that's it. Lower 'im now, hurry!"

Slim let the loose line snake through his hands at moderate speed, and the limp form of the crossbreed lowered toward the waiting men Andy and Dee had tied the hounds to a nearby tree, and now they barked and bellowed in their eagerness to get at the cat

As soon as the lowering animal reached them, Dee tied a length of cord snugly around the front feet while Andy did the same with the hind paws. Not until then did they signal Slim to lower the animal the rest of the way to the ground As soon as the line went slack, Slim dropped the trailing end off to one side, tossed the pole down carefully away from them in another direction and himself started descending.

Just as soon as slack had formed in the rope, Dee jerked the noose away from the 'at's neck and clapped over the crossbreed's head a leather pouch with draw-strings at the opening and several dime-sized air holes near the end He tightened the drawstrings and tied them securely enough to hold the bag in place, but not so tightly that the animal could not breathe. By the time he was finished, Slim was just reaching the ground, panting heavily and his deep-set eyes were afire with excitement He ran over to where the men were kneeling beside the crossbreed and grinned.

"How'd I do, Dee, huh? How'd I do?"

"You done good, Slim Real good."

" 'Cat make it 'live?"

"Sure 'nuff." Dee motioned with his thumb at the crossbreed, wh se sides were heaving convulsively. A hacking, choking series of gasps, muffled by the leather hood, were becoming audible. "He only lost one of his lives a-hangin' there. Reckon he's got eight more left "

All three men laughed. Then, with Dee holding the crossbreed's front legs and silent Andy the rear, the pair started toward the truck. The triumphant Slim, still grinning broadly, trailed behind and struggled to hold the straining dogs, the rope, the pole and three rifles.

XIV

Big Art Fay, it was rumored, had the uncanny knack
for making money from whatever he touched or, for
that matter, whatever touched him. Once, so the story
went, when he had slyly bilked an acquaintance out of
a sizable sum, the latter had angrily punched Fay in the
mouth and then stormed away. Whereupon Fay gingerly reached into his own mouth to remove what he
thought was a chunk of broken tooth and found that it
was a four-carat diamond from the man's ring. Somehow, it seemed, no matter what Fay did, he made
money from it.

The rumor went even further: it said that he had
never earned a dollar legally in his life.

The adjective "Big" in front of Art Fay's name was
not due so much to his size—though he was decidedly
fat—as it was to his power in a number of fields: local
politics, housing, construction, insurance, moneylending
and various and sundry other occupations.

He was very well known within that triangle formed
by the three cities of Pine Bluff, Hot Springs and Little
Rock, and there were few activities going on—
clandestine or otherwise—in which he didn't have his
chubby fingers. He was, above all, a gambler and he

saw to it unfailingly that the odds were always well stacked in his own favor.

When Dee, Slim and Andy approached him in Pine Bluff with the captive crossbreed snarling and spitting in a wire cage, he immediately saw a monetary potential in the creature. True to form, however, he did not let on and shook his head sadly at their request for fifty dollars for the animal. The bobcat wasn't the biggest he'd ever seen, he told them, and its coloring was off, meaning it was probably sickly or a freak. But, realizing what the trio went through to catch it and sympathetic for their efforts, he "allowed as to how" he might give them thirty dollars for it.

The three men accepted the offer with ill-concealed glee, certain that they had finally pulled one off on Big Art Fay. They would have sold the crossbreed to him for fifteen dollars if it had come to that. Fay, on the other hand, accepted the animal with well-concealed delight; he would have paid up to a hundred dollars before letting it get away from him.

For the crossbreed himself, it was a bad time. His throat was swollen and painful and he was both hungry and thirsty, having been given neither food nor water in the two days since his capture. Dogs had slavered near his cage and tore at it in an attempt to get at him, terrifying him, and a little boy had amused himself for nearly an hour by poking a stick through the wires at him in an effort to gouge an eye. Only a healthy swat on the side of the boy's head by Dee had saved the crossbreed's eyesight. And now, nervous, frightened, angry, hungry and thirsty, the crossbreed snarled and hissed and spat at anything which moved within five feet of his cage. Big Art Fay nodded approvingly.

For twelve days more the crossbreed remained in the slightly roomier and better-constructed cage in a shed to which Fay's men had transferred him. Once a day he was fed a large bowlful of coarsely ground meat and a coffee can was kept filled with water for him to drink. Otherwise, he was left relatively to himself.

By the end of the first couple of days, every fraction

of an inch of the interior of the cage had been inspected thoroughly by the animal, but it was constructed of strong wire and metal posts, impervious to the attacks of his teeth and claws, and he soon realized the futility of tearing or biting at it.

On the thirteenth day his cage was unceremoniously loaded into the back end of a pickup truck, covered with a dusty tarpaulin and driven just over seventy miles to a surprisingly well-constructed little arena in the resort city of Hot Springs. Two of Fay's helpers carried the cage inside the concrete-walled, circular pit area, and from all around them there was a continuing bedlam of noises from the bleacher-seated crowd here assembled. Men dressed in expensive suits and ladies in finery and glittering with gems sat on the hard seats beside grizzled farmers and laborers clad in patched dungarees.

In the center of the pit was a circular wire pen, perhaps nine feet in diameter and five feet high, covered on the top with the same strong wire which made up the sides. Two small doors leading into this pen faced each other from opposing sides, and it was to one of these that the crossbreed's cage was carried. In a moment it had been neatly attached to the larger pen in such a manner that when the sliding door was raised, he would have access to the bigger enclosure.

In a few moments another cage was brought in. It contained an ugly white mongrel dog, a bit larger than the crossbreed, its face crisscrossed with a network of scars, some of them black with age and others an angry pink and relatively fresh.

The babble of voices from the crowd became harsher now as numbers were called back and forth and bets placed. The white dog was well known here. He had been pitted against numerous raccoons and cats, once against an eagle and another time against a medium-sized badger. The fact that he was still fighting attested to his success in his previous battles.

In those contests—particularly those in which he had been pitted against house cats—he had been expected to win, and the betting was based not so much on whether or not he would emerge victorious, but rather on how long it would take him to make the kill. On the wall of this pit was mounted a large timing clock which recorded in lights the passage of seconds and minutes.

While this ugly mongrel had not previously been pitted against a bobcat—or a crossbreed—nevertheless, he was an odds-on favorite to win the forthcoming fight. The size and apparent viciousness of his adversary, however, caused much of the betting to be simply on which animal would kill the other, rather than on the time it would take to do it.

Big Art Fay was not overly concerned about what the final results would be. He half expected the cat to be killed but, even in this event, he still stood to make several hundred dollars from the match. And if, by some chance, the cat happened to emerge victorious, he would win upwards of a thousand dollars. If nothing else, Big Art Fay was a shrewd gambler.

The house lights were dimmed except for a set of floodlights which overhung the pen and illuminated it harshly. The babbling of the crowd died away and an aura of vibrant expectancy filled the arena. Fay's man moved to the crossbreed's cage, raised the door and then, with a sharp stick, prodded the animal until he leaped out into the more expansive pen and crouched there snarling, his tail twitching rapidly. As soon as he was out, the cage door closed behind him.

A moment later the door of the dog's pen was similarly opened, and a roar erupted from the spectators as the animal charged out without the encouragement of prodding, knowing well what was in store and eager for the battle. He ran directly toward the crouching crossbreed whose whole attention was now riveted to him. Neither animal paid any attention to the closing of the dog's pen door or the noisiness of the crowd. Nothing existed now for either but his adversary.

As the dog charged in a ferocious first onslaught that had usually overwhelmed any opponent and marked an early beginning of the end, the crossbreed neatly sidestepped and flung out a widespread paw with its claws fully bared. The dog turned his gaping jaws to follow the crossbreed's move, but missed by a mere inch.

The crossbreed did not.

His claws dug deeply into the mongrel's snout and tore fiercely, severing the strip of flesh which separated the dog's nostrils. The rip continued down through the dog's upper lip, and when both combatants regained their balance and poised momentarily facing each other at a distance of several feet, the dog's snout was bleeding profusely and his mouth was flecked with red foam.

Both animals were snarling fiercely and using the brief pause to estimate the opponent's vulnerability. The crowd shrieked, and now another flurry of betting was begun; and though the dog was still favored to win, the odds in his favor had decreased considerably.

Again he charged the crossbreed and this time succeeded in bowling him over. His teeth closed momentarily on the cat's right ear and ripped through it; but the teeth of the crossbreed also found their mark, biting deeply into the upper muscle of the dog's foreleg. The mongrel yelped sharply, released the crossbreed's ear and bit at the body of his opponent. The teeth closed on the cat's flank, puncturing the flesh painfully, but not tearing through muscle tissue or vital organs.

Once more they broke apart, and suddenly it was no longer the dog who was the aggressor. The crossbreed flung himself at the white mongrel who raised on his hind legs to meet the attack. They clinched, both standing high on their hind feet and then they toppled over in a thrashing mass. The dog's mouth had closed on the side of the crossbreed's neck, but the fur was thick there and the skin loose, and once again he did little permanent damage. He seemed unable to contend with the cat's incredibly swift reflexes.

The crossbreed's teeth had fastened securely in the dog's throat, and his front paws had encircled the larger animal's neck. And now came into play his deadliest tactic. Pumping his hind legs savagely, he unleashed the powerful curved claws of his hind feet, and these claws dug deeply into the belly of the dog from rib cage to groin. Time after time they ripped into the flesh, tearing away fur and skin and then even abdominal muscle tissue.

The dog's snarling became a howl of pain and terror and now he flung himself about haphazardly, unable to get his slavering jaws on this animal and desperately trying to dislodge him. But with the tenaciousness of a leech, the crossbreed retained his grip with teeth and front claws, while his rear claws continued to rip and shred his enemy's soft underside.

Suddenly those claws tore a great rip in the thin stomach muscles, and the entrails of the dog bulged outward. Still the cat's claws worked and the intestines tore and spilled their grisly contents to the arena floor. Even then the crossbreed maintained his hold and his slashing claws caused the entrails to part. Sections of them trailed out, wrapped around the dog's own feet and his frantic struggling pulled them out even farther.

A breathless silence now prevailed over the spectators, broken only by the labored breathing and the low, strangled growlings of the combatants. The white dog was weakening rapidly.

A sudden gush of blood from the gaping wound mingled with the torn viscera, and the floor of the arena became slick with the foul mess. Nevertheless, the mongrel began to run in blind panic. He crashed glancingly into the wire wall of the pen, knocking himself down; but it was the crossbreed who had taken the brunt of the collision with the hard wire. It had caught him on the side of the head, and he was knocked free of the dog. Instantly, even though he was dazed and his vision foggy, he sped across the pen as far as he could get from the dog and crouched, awaiting the next onslaught.

The expected attack did not materialize.

The mongrel, moving in a distinctly uncoordinated manner, managed to reach the closed doorway leading to his own cage. Here he stood silently for a few seconds, his body shaking convulsively, until his hind-

quarters collapsed. For a few seconds more he managed to hold himself upright on his forelegs, but then they too gave way and he rolled over onto his side. He kicked spastically a few times, heaved a great moaning sigh and then lay still.

The white dog was dead.

A collective pent-up breath escaped the crowd, and one of the well-dressed ladies, holding a gloved hand to her mouth, stumbled toward the exit with the aid of her escort. In the front row of the bleachers, Dee, Andy and Slim sat frozen, the latter white-faced and as shaken as he'd ever been before, reliving in a new light his close contact with this savage cat high in the oak tree.

Dee shook his head in wonderment and muttered, "There goes our thirty bucks." They had bet on the dog.

Andy, as usual, said nothing, but Slim nodded. His Adam's apple bobbed furiously, and abruptly he got to his feet and lurched toward the exit. In a moment Dee and Andy followed him, Dee still shaking his head.

Big Art Fay, grinning jubilantly, gave instructions to his helpers and then turned away to collect his winnings. As customary, whatever he put his hand to made money for him. His thirty-dollar investment had become an extremely good one, and this was only a start.

The two helpers went to the arena pen, opened the crossbreed's cage door and then prodded at him with long poles until they had forced him back into it. Then they secured the door and carried the cage out to their waiting truck, covering it, as they had before, with the heavy tarpaulin. Inside this enclosed darkness the crossbreed crouched in one corner of the cage, waves of uncontrollable trembling rippling his body. His heart was still hammering heavily, and a low mournful moaning sound escaped him.

Back in the pit area of the arena, attendants had removed the mutilated body of the white dog and were spreading sawdust over the ugly mess on the floor. From cages in several other rooms the muted din of barkings and growlings, snarlings and yowls of other animals who would soon be having their turns in the pit reached the spectators still in their seats. Somehow, though, whatever came now could not help to be rather anticlimactic, and a portion of the crowd began drifting out of the exits.

Outside the arena door, Dee was talking with Big Art Fay, while a short distance from them Andy and Slim waited. Fay was shaking his head with what appeared to be sincere sympathy as he listened to what Dee had to say.

"It's tough," he admitted when Dee paused, "but I can't help the way you men bet. Feller that bets against his own man, so to speak, is apt to get into trouble." He chuckled and his eyes became rather distant as a thought struck him: it was altogether possible that sometime in the future these men might bring him another bobcat and he wanted to encourage such a possibility. He smiled and nodded. "Tell you what, though, Dee. Just to show you I'm a fair man, I'll give you the price you originally asked for that 'cat."

He removed a well-padded wallet from his pocket, extracted a ten-dollar bill and two fives and handed them to Dee. He winked, and then his eyes glinted with conspiratorial approval as Dee folded the ten and slipped it into his shirt pocket before beckoning his companions to come over. When they did, he handed them each a five-dollar bill.

"Mr. Fay done give us a little to sort of make up for what we lost," he explained. "Sure do thank you, Art."

Big Art Fay smiled benignly. "Hang onto that money, boys, and wait'll you hear the word. In a week or so we'll have that 'cat up in Little Rock for another bout. Take my advice and bet on him this time."

XV

For the next two weeks the crossbreed remained in the cage within Big Art Fay's shed in Pine Bluff. His neck and side, where the white dog had bitten him, were very painful, and it seemed that every muscle in his body ached when he moved.

It had taken three days for him to recover from the shock and fright of the encounter, and at the end of that time he had taken up pacing fretfully in the limited confines of his pen. He could move only two steps in any one direction, but by staying close to the walls of the cage and continuing to turn, he could walk.

Hour after hour he would pad silently in this fashion, sometimes moving clockwise, sometimes counterclockwise. The heavy pine planking, which was the floor of the pen, took on a smooth polished appearance where his feet paced off the endless miles of confined walking.

For days after the battle he was extremely nervous and only gradually did he settle down and return to a semblance of normality. His only significant physical injury was the torn right ear. The teeth of the white dog had bitten through it close to the base and had torn a considerable rip in it before the hold was released. Fortunately, the rip did not extend all the way out to the edge of the ear or it would have healed in two parts rather than one. As it was, the edges of the gash had closed together well, sealed with scabrous material, and the wound was slowly healing. He would have a scar, but not even a very noticeable one at that.

His naturally savage nature had not mellowed since his capture and had, in fact, become more pronounced since the fight in Hot Springs. When the water or food bowls were pushed through the narrow gap in the wiring with a stick or taken away, he would attack the wood fiercely, biting it and snarling and, when this availed him nothing, he would fling himself bodily at the wiring, causing the person outside the cage to flinch and draw back respectfully.

Big Art Fay was delighted with this display. It assured him that the animal would more than ever put on a good show at the next match. It was a match already arranged to be held in a supposedly secret, but nevertheless well-known, converted-barn arena on the northern outskirts of Little Rock.

The alleged sport of baiting—pitting game cocks, wild animals, domestic animals or combinations of these against each other in mortal combat—was illegal here, just as practically everywhere else in the nation, but it was carried on to a considerable degree despite the laws. Now and then the authorities would order token raids but well-placed bribes took care of any serious threat from the law. The baitings were overlooked as long as they were not too flauntingly staged.

The organizers of these baitings—of which Big Art Fay was a prime force—and the owners of the combatants were normally the money-holders for most of the over-the-board betting. If, as sometimes occurred, the police closed in, then the organizer was held responsible for the monies lost or confiscated. By the same token, if an owner failed to produce the scheduled combatant or if that animal refused to fight or if the battle was in any way forfeit, then the other combatant was automatically victor, and the owner of the defaulter was obliged to pay the losses.

About this, Big Art Fay was little concerned. He had been assured there would be no raid and he had no doubt whatever that his newest acquisition would put up as spectacular a fight as anyone could hope for. He was well aware that in the days since the white dog had been killed, the fame of the "striped bobcat," as his entry was being called, had spread widely. Even though death was more the rule than the exception in the baiting pit, it had rarely—if ever—been occasioned with such dramatic unexpectedness and harshness as in the fight between the crossbreed and the white mongrel.

The tale of that fight was passed by word of mouth until few bettors throughout most of central Arkansas, and particularly in the heavily populated triangle of the three cities, had not heard all of the grisly details. When further word spread that another such conflict was to be staged, this time between the striped bobcat and a huge redbone hound noted for his many kills of cats in the pit, betting began a week before the fight was scheduled.

On the evening of the match, Big Art Fay smiled approvingly at Dee, Slim and Andy as the trio made their bets in favor of the crossbreed at the arena; and as soon as they had gone to take their seats, he placed over $1,000 in bets himself . . . and every penny of it on the redbone hound.

Notwithstanding the ferocity of this cat, Fay had no illusions that it could win over the famed redbone. This was not a dog that would allow himself to be so readily disemboweled. Not only did he outweigh the crossbreed by at least fifty pounds, but he was a dog that had been bred to be a killer—a dog that rarely took over three minutes to kill the cat against which he was pitted; a dog that had more than once been shipped to Arizona or Utah or Texas to engage in lion hunts when a cougar had turned stock killer.

Even standing room was at a premium at the arena this night, and though several bouts were scheduled before the crossbreed's, it was his that had drawn the crowds and which was the featured attraction of the night. The smell of blood was in the air.

In the first three scheduled fights, a Walker hound and two husky mongrels had made short work of three cats; none had survived for more than ten minutes, though one of the mongrels had incurred a shredded ear in the process. The fourth match was mostly for entertainment, and little betting was done on it except by novices: a free-for-all match in which six cats were pitted against three dogs. It was pure carnage, heightened by the fact that, after the cats had been killed, two of the dogs turned on the third and killed him as well.

After those matches the center pen was cleaned and fresh sawdust spread. Then the cages of the redbone hound and the crossbreed were put into place against the larger pen.

The general undertone of bettors' voices gradually diminished and at last the main lights were lowered. For the fifth time this evening the arena floodlights spread their harsh glare over the center pen. The crossbreed was prodded out of his cage and the sliding door shut behind him. He crouched silently against it, his chin nearly on the floor and his slitted eyes locked on the little door across the pen which at this moment the handlers were raising.

As the huge head of the dog pushed under the partially raised sliding door in his eagerness to get out, the door jammed and momentarily held him. Terrorized at the size of this hound, the crossbreed yowled loudly. As the handlers fumbled to free the door, it moved a little farther up and then stuck again halfway open. The redbone hound virtually lay on his side as he squeezed out from under it. Growling savagely, he braced his hind feet against the door and thrust against it, freeing himself but shoving his cage loose from its moorings on the center pen. Instantly he charged the crossbreed. The cat waited until the last possible moment and then streaked to one side with an incredible burst of speed, raced in a half-circle around the pen with the dog on his heels and plunged under the still partially open door into the smaller cage the dog had just left behind.

The hound slammed headlong into the door, and with a screeching sound the smaller cage broke away from its moorings entirely and flipped completely over. Even as the cage was rolling to a stop, the crossbreed sped out of it. Two doorways led out of the concrete-walled arena, and into one of these the crossbreed lunged while startled handlers and spectators scattered as if a lion had suddenly broken loose.

The hound recovered himself quickly and plunged after the crossbreed, no more than fifteen feet behind him; but now the advantage belonged to the cat. Amid screams and bellows from the crowd pressed about the doors, he raced easily through the jungle of legs. The dog also pushed his way through, but he had a harder time of it and at times his scruff was momentarily gripped roughly until he could break free.

Several people in the crowd fell, and a near panic erupted; but by then the crossbreed was outside in the darkness and racing down the aisle of a large, thoroughly filled parking lot. The dog was still following, but had lost distance because of the interceptions and interference he had run through. More than fifty feet separated the two animals now.

Though the fear was still strong in him, a sense of exultation bloomed in the crossbreed. He scrambled swiftly under three cars, then slipped through a gap in a board fence. It was a narrow opening, and he very nearly got stuck. Frantically he strained and shoved and abruptly popped to the other side just as the redbone hound caught up to him. The dog thrust his head through the gap and his bite just barely touched the fur of the crossbreed's rump as he bounded away.

The dog struggled furiously to get through and then, realizing he couldn't, pulled his head back and began racing down the length of the fence in the direction he had seen the crossbreed disappear in the darkness. The cat had been too wily to continue running in that direction, however. As soon as the hound vanished from view behind the fence, the crossbreed turned sharply and began running diagonally away in the opposite direction.

Far behind him he could still hear screaming, and a general uproar in the arena, but he paid them no attention. Then he also heard the baying of the hound, and this most assuredly concerned him; he would have to use every bit of his cunning to throw this experienced dog off his trail.

He was running in a field now through which a deep erosion gully meandered. In the bottom of the gully was an inch or so of slowly flowing water, and he leaped into it without hesitation. He ran downstream in the water for several hundred yards before scrambling back up the bank and continuing his cross-country run toward the northeast. Behind him the baying—now with a frustrated ring to it as the hound tried to unravel the water-interrupted trail—grew fainter.

Within ten minutes he encountered a small creek and again he plunged into the water, this time working his way upstream for some distance. The sound of the baying behind him had quickened—the hound had found where the crossbreed had left the erosion gully. In another moment the cat came to where a smaller rill joined the stream he had been following. He turned and raced upstream here, leaping on a fallen tree that lay partially in the water. He ran upwards toward the roots and, at the top of the bank, flung himself off in a great leap which spanned twenty feet.

When he alighted, he leaped again, this time at an angle to the first jump, and then a third time, each of the last two bounds covering eight or ten feet. Then he settled down to a hard, steady run. Far ahead of him was the dense shadow of a deep woods. When he reached it, he paused again and listened. The baying, again with a puzzled note to it, was now coming from approximately where he had entered the creek.

Though he was probably safe now against the hound's figuring out his maneuver there, the crossbreed still had a stratagem or two to perform. At the same time he was keenly watchful of where he was going and wary lest he happen to run into unforeseen danger. There was a zigzagging, interlocked rail fence, about four feet high, running along the edge of the woodland, and he leaped over it easily without touching it. He ran directly into the woods a dozen yards or more to a large tree, circled it, climbed about ten feet up the trunk and then came down again. At once he turned and retraced his own steps to the fence and paused there, again listening.

The baying of the hound was still audible, but if anything, farther away than last time. He bunched his muscles and sprang twelve feet to one side parallel with the fence, hit the ground and sprang again, this time to the top rail of the barrier. With perfect balance and ease he raced along the top of the fence for over two hundred feet and then leaped from it to the trunk of a slender sapling six feet away. He climbed it until it bowed sharply with his weight away from the fence, dropped lightly to the ground and trotted into the woods, no longer making any attempt to hide his trail. If and when the redbone hound managed to unravel the mystery of his movements this far, he would by then be many miles away.

Throughout the night he continued moving northeastward at that mile-eating pace, occasionally obliterating his trail by traveling short distances through the shallow waters of creek shores. During the night he paused only three times: twice to catch a total of five meadow voles, and once to drink and briefly rest beside a meandering stream. By the time the first faint suggestion of dawn was illuminating the eastern horizon, he was easily twenty-five miles away from the converted-barn arena outside Little Rock.

Here, well hidden in brush beside the trunk of a large wind-uprooted tree, he settled down for the day and slept. And for the first time in nearly a month his slumber was deep and undisturbed by the movements of his most implacable enemy—man.

XVI

Throughout the summer the crossbreed continued a leisurely but steady progress to the north. At least once or twice each day he would pause and stand for long periods with his muzzle raised high, sniffing the air, again to the north. The peculiar drive that compelled him to travel in this direction he did not understand; he only accepted it and followed it automatically.

He moved with great caution always, but especially when he came in closer contact with urban areas. Time after time he had been chased by dogs, sometimes with men as well. But now he learned his lesson; he never treed if it could be avoided. He became even more skilled at eluding such pursuit, and not once was he ever really in jeopardy. Twice, during the summer, guns had barked at him with shattering unexpectedness: once the shots had missed and another time he had been stung sharply but not seriously by shotgun pellets. Such incidents only made him all the more cautious in his movements.

More often than not he traveled by night rather than by day, hunting wherever he encountered prey and feeding very well. By the time he had entered south-central Missouri, his diet was predominantly cottontail

rabbits, for in this scrub-oak country there was an incredible abundance of these rodents. Frequently he encountered foxes, occasionally other bobcats and twice coyotes, all engaged in hunting the same prey; but mostly they ignored each other and went their own ways.

His hunting prowess became highly advanced and he could trail, stalk or pursue with equal skill. His diet came to include ground squirrels and chipmunks, occasional woodchucks and quail, frogs and snakes, squirrels and mice. And once he killed an injured fawn in a rocky creekbed, where for two days it had been lying, growing progressively weaker, its front hoof wedged inextricably between two rocks and its shinbone broken.

His senses of smell, sight and hearing became even more acute and highly adept at detecting either enemy or prey. And he continued to grow. By the time the first frosts of autumn had set fire to the leaves of maples and oaks and gum trees, the crossbreed was thirty-four inches long, stood fourteen inches at the shoulder and weighed thirty-three pounds. He was uncommonly handsome, with widely-flaring cheek tufts and long sensitive whiskers which extended on both sides of the cheek tufts by a half inch or more. His body was lithe and strong, and he could run for hours at top speed or all day at a rapid trot, if need be.

He climbed with great facility and moved about in the branches of trees with very nearly the agility of a squirrel and, not unexpectedly—since he was, after all, a cat—he retained his tremendous curiosity. It was this latter trait, in fact, which more than once led him into difficulty.

One time, in order to search out the source of a compelling scent, he poked his head into a small hollow, well up in an oak tree, ignoring the fact that his whiskers touched wood on both sides. His head became wedged in the opening, and though he struggled to free himself, he was stuck.

The source of the odd scent was the musk of a least weasel, himself following the spoor of a flying squirrel.

When the head of the crossbreed blocked the exit—a head almost as broad as the weasel's entire six inches of body length—the weasel had drawn back and crouched fearfully against the farthest reaches of the little hollow. A ferocious little creature in his own right, he snarled shrilly at the struggling cat, then suddenly darted forward and dauntlessly buried his sharp teeth in the crossbreed's tender nose.

Surprised and pained, the crossbreed gave a great jerk backwards and his head popped free of the hole. He lost his balance and fell thirty feet to the ground where, slightly winded but otherwise unhurt, he looked up at the weasel peeking from the hollow. Oblivious of the fact that the bite of the little creature might have saved his life, he snarled briefly, licked his injured nose and trotted off.

Though he continued to travel in a generally northward direction, there were times when natural or man-made barriers forced him to swing widely off course. One such case occurred where he encountered the wide Missouri River just a few miles west of Jefferson City. He might have followed the eastward flow of the current toward its junction with the Mississippi River well over a hundred miles downstream from here, but with populous Jefferson City in the way, he turned instead to the west and followed relatively near to the shoreline as the river swung gradually north.

At the village of Glasgow, where the Missouri River turned sharply west again, he slunk across the highway bridge, unnoticed in the dead of night. Close by, entering the Missouri from the north, was the Chariton River, and so now he began following the course of that stream. Twelve days later, when he reached the point where this river also veered almost due west at Chariton, Iowa, he left the watercourse and continued overland to the northwest. On the fourth day of traveling after that, he encountered the Racoon River within sight of the sprawling capital city of Des Moines.

Again he was inclined to turn eastward, and, as before, the prospect of approaching any nearer a populous area changed his mind and he followed the Raccoon River upstream, first southwestwardly, but then in a great arc which gradually straightened out toward a northwestward origin.

Game was plentiful along the course of this river, and while still he preyed most consistently upon rabbits and mice, he now found himself in an area where large and delicious ringneck pheasants were in abundance, and not infrequently he caught and ate them. Still he did not stop, driven ever onward by his compulsive urge.

Now he encountered the only snow he had ever seen. A fearful storm swept up out of the Western Plains and struck just about the time he reached the Cottonwood River of southwestern Minnesota. Temperatures plummeted far below freezing, and for three days the snow fell. The crossbreed holed up within the bole of a large stump still thrusting ten or twelve feet above the ground. The base of the den was thick with dried leaves, and its opening, four feet above, was to the leeward of prevailing winds. It was a comfortable and safe location, and so, for the first time since his long overland journey began last spring, the crossbreed seemed relatively content to remain where he was.

As autumn moved into winter, his striped coat thickened and the fur of his legs became much denser. It gave the queer illusion that he had greatly increased in size, even though his weight had remained almost the same. He appeared to revel in the crispness of the biting winter air and at times romped through shoulder-deep snow with all the playfulness and abandon of a kitten. He delighted in pawing through it, sniffing the fresh, warm scent of mice along their tunneled runs through leaves and weed debris buried under the white blanket.

He had to hunt a little harder in these times in order to catch his food, but there were few days when he was not successful enough in his hunting to satisfy himself. Often, when he nabbed prey unexpectedly at times when he was not particularly hungry, he would bury it under leaves or snow or even in his own den and save it for a later time when food might be harder to come by.

In addition to an abundance of mice and cottontail rabbits here, he was now back in the territory that not only supported a large pheasant population, but a very substantial number of snowshoe rabbits as well. These rabbits were more difficult to capture than their smaller cottontail cousins, but since they were so much larger they lasted longer as food.

The crossbreed could often pursue and run down a cottontail rabbit in the snow, but the larger rabbit could escape him easily. As its name suggested, its hind feet were broad and almost six inches long and acted much like snowshoes, allowing it to race swiftly across the surface of lightly crusted snow into which the crossbreed sank deeply at each step.

Stealth, therefore, became the necessary ingredient in capturing the nimble creatures, along with the ability to sense their presence before they sensed him. This in itself was difficult, since the snowshoe rabbit had another important advantage: its color in summer was very similar to that of the cottontail, but in winter it became pure white except for the very tips of its ears, which were black. Against a background of snow, with its ears flattened against the fur of its back, the snowshoe rabbit was so well camouflaged that it could remain almost invisible, even at close range.

When, in late December, a wave of polar air spread southward over the area—the temperature dropped to twenty degrees below zero and for six days did not again climb above the zero mark even in daytime—food became critically scarce. During much of this time the crossbreed remained in his den sleeping, but at last hunger drove him to hunt. Not unexpectedly, little prey was available. The ground had frozen so solidly that he could not begin to paw through it as he had done previously in his search for mice. Even the snow had become so crusted that he could run along its surface without breaking through; but now that he could do this, the rabbits—both cottontails and snow-shoes—had seemingly become nonexistent.

On a hunt one bitterly cold night, he spied a large cock pheasant, hunkered in a little declivity of the snow beside a log. Instantly he flattened and made a stealthy circle around the log, so that he was hidden from view and the wind was in his favor.

When he was as close as he could approach without being seen, he suddenly lunged over the log and pounced on the bird, claws and teeth grasping it simultaneously. He was momentarily taken aback when the bird didn't even move, and then he realized that it was dead. Wounded by hunters the day before, it had found this hiding place in which to crouch and die. Its flesh was now frozen hard as stone, and the expression of the crossbreed was almost comical as he stepped back and cocked his head to look at this bird poised so lifelike even in death.

It was an even more ludicrous situation an instant later when he picked up the big bird in his mouth and trotted with it to his nearby den. He leaped to the entrance, dropped lightly inside, then quickly scraped a hole in the leaves and debris at the bottom. He placed the bird in it and then covered it. Hungry though he was, he would first try to capture some living meat and save this bird for later, in the event that his hunt was not successful.

A few minutes later he was ranging again in a wide half-circle which took him four or five miles away. Throughout the night he padded about, and only once in those hours did he come across prey: a cottontail rabbit which burst into a frenzied run from beside a tree twenty feet ahead and managed to keep ahead of him until it plunged out of sight in a labyrinth of passages within a huge pile of tangled driftwood beside the frozen river.

Now it was breaking dawn, and he was just on the verge of returning to his den when, a quarter mile from the little town of Sanborn, the scent of fresh meat struck his nostrils with almost the impact of a physical blow. Head held high and nostrils working carefully with faint little sniffings, he followed the airborne scent toward the town.

Despite his hunger, despite the wonderful aroma of the meat, he moved cautiously and keenly, alert for any movement which might suggest danger; but there was none. The aroma drew him toward an outlying farmyard where a cluster of buildings loomed clearly in the half-light. It was near the base of a huge skeletal cottonwood tree, not more than a hundred yards from the farmhouse, where he found the source of the scent.

Though he could not see the meat itself, the aroma of it was emanating from a hollow at the base of the tree, and the meat was obviously inside. This hollow was large enough for a small raccoon or fox to squeeze its forequarters inside, but it was much too small for the crossbreed. He crouched close in front of it and felt inward with one forepaw. With a bit of fumbling he was successful in reaching the chunk of partially frozen meat, and he hooked it neatly with a sharp curved claw.

As he began to draw it toward him, the meat pulled out of his grasp, and he fumbled for it again with the extended paw. Simultaneously there came a sharp snapping sound and a terrible pain which ran up his front leg. He lurched away fearfully and was less than two feet from the tree when the biting pressure on his right foot stopped him so abruptly that his body turned a flip. He landed on his back while another severe wave of pain ran up his leg and caused him to moan in anguish.

The steel trap, set to catch a raccoon, had nabbed him instead. Its powerful jaws had snapped over the center two toes of his foot, and the lunge that had flipped him over on his back broke the bones in both of these toes. Snarling, he bit at the metal, but only hurt his mouth and lost part of his tongue skin when it stuck to the frigid steel.

Again he tried to pull away and again he was held fast, lost his balance and fell to his side. His hind claws ripped at the trap now, but made no more headway against it than his teeth had. A length of chain stretched from the trap to the tree, to which its terminal ring was securely nailed in place with three heavy fencing staples. There was no possibility that he could pull the trap away.

The pain was excruciating, and the two center toes were now stretched an abnormal distance from the rest of his foot. An involuntary yowl of pain left him and carried a considerable distance in the crisp, early morning air. In answer, there came from the nearby barnyard the barking of a dog. The crossbreed stifled his own cry in the middle and stared fearfully in that direction, but the damage had been done.

The dog was a nondescript mongrel, chained to a large shedlike doghouse close to the back door of the farmhouse. Now, as he raced back and forth within the radius of his tether and continued his wild barking, the door opened briefly. A bathrobe-clad youth of about sixteen stuck his head out and called at the dog to be quiet. The dog paid no attention to him and continued to pull against the chain and bark with frantic hoarseness in the direction of the big cottonwood tree. Though it was hardly likely that he saw the crossbreed, the boy seemed suddenly to understand what had happened and he ducked back into the house.

Deeply afraid now, the crossbreed lunged again and again against the trap, ignoring the dreadful waves of pain which surged up his trapped leg. Still he couldn't pull free, and in a final desperate effort he began biting the flesh of his own imprisoned foot. Though the pain must have been intense, no further sound came from him. In moments he had bitten much of the stretched flesh away, and his toes were now attached to his foot largely by the strong white tendons.

At the house the door slammed, and the crossbreed looked up to see the youth, clad in a heavy coat with parka, fumbling with the collar of the prancing dog.

In desperation the crossbreed gave another strong lunge. It caused the tendons and remaining flesh of his toes to part, and just that suddenly he was free of the trap. Though weak from pain and his exertions, he raced away toward the fringe of woods which marked the frozen course of the Cottonwood River. Surprisingly, he used the injured foot with scarcely a limp.

Behind him the boy was still attempting to free the dog and was obviously being hampered by the energetic bounding of the animal. Not until the crossbreed had almost reached the woods did the dog come galloping over the snow-covered field toward the trap site, the boy running far behind him.

At first, the blood from the crossbreed's foot stained the snow at every leap, but this quickly stopped and little trace of his passage showed on the hard crust. Nevertheless, if the dog was a good trailer, the cat was still in serious trouble.

The dog was a good watchdog and a fine pet, but he was by no means a good hunter and an even worse tracker. Until the boy arrived, he sniffed excitedly about the tree and especially at the trap still containing the two toes; but though his young master urged him to range out and follow the escaped quarry, the dog seemed not to understand what was desired of him. He stayed close to the boy.

Already a half mile away and hidden from view by the river trees, the crossbreed raced along on the crusted snow covering the ice, veering now and then to run skiddingly along extensive narrow patches where winds had swept the river ice free of its covering. Even a good tracker would have difficulty following him over this.

Three-quarters of an hour later, the crossbreed leaped up and into his den stump and flopped to the leaves below, his sides heaving; and, for the first time since the dog had begun barking, a low whine issued from his mouth.

At once he began licking his injured paw, which was now hot with inflammation and beginning to swell very badly. For three hours without pause he licked it. Though this eased the pain somewhat, when he tried to

stand, he found that the leg would scarcely support his weight.

The fortunate happenstance that had led him to conceal the frozen pheasant in his den before continuing last night's hunt was now an unanticipated blessing. With some difficulty he nosed away the leaves, uncovering the bird, and then began to tear at it with his teeth, holding it down with his uninjured forepaw. The feathers pulled out easily, but it took considerable chewing and painful tugging for him to begin jerking small chunks of the frozen meat away.

Difficult though it may have been to gnaw and eat, it *was* food and it would sustain him, and he was very lucky indeed. It would be a long while before he would again be able to hunt with any degree of his previous skill and success.

XVII

The remainder of the winter was difficult for the cross-breed. Though within a week he was limping about and able to catch occasional mice and, once, a cottontail rabbit—which probably could have escaped by dashing away, but merely sat there petrified when the cross-breed charged—it was easily a month before he was able to move about again with reasonable balance, speed and skill.

His track in the snow was now two-toed rather than four- and very distinctive in its appearance. The foot itself looked peculiar, with no toes in the center and two on the edges, but the wound had healed well. A trailing piece of tendon had dried up along with the damaged flesh and eventually fell away under the ministrations of his rasping tongue. The dense fur on his foot had closed over the wound and now it was hardly recognizable as an old wound. Actually, it appeared more like a congenital malformation.

That it had somehow affected his hunting was obvious. He was required to work harder to catch less, and more than one mouse or rabbit had escaped his grasp when, by rights, it should have been caught by the two missing-claws. So by now, in the waning weeks of winter, though he was once again essentially well and able to fend for himself without undue difficulty, the effect of his ordeal was apparent. His fur was not as prime and lustrous as it should have been, and he had lost so much weight—almost five pounds—that his pelt seemed to be merely draped over his frame rather than an integral part of his anatomy.

As soon as he had become able to walk again and run rapidly, should such necessity be forced upon him, the urge to wander had built up within him. Once more he began his generally northward peregrination. He took his time, rarely traveling more than ten miles in any one day, and so it was the first week of April before he encountered a significant milestone in his journey. At a sleepy city named Little Falls he came to a river. It was a relatively good-sized one, fairly wide, clear and cold, and a very attractive stream.

It was the Mississippi River.

At this point he was still a considerable distance from its headwaters in Lake Itasca, but the river here bore little resemblance to the broad and muddy current he had twice ridden and nearly drowned in so long ago. It was just after dawn that he reached this point, and with no more particular attention to it than he had paid to any other stream he had encountered, he quickly loped across the sturdy bridge and followed the east bank of the stream southward until he had left behind him the buildings of Little Falls.

It was hardly likely that he recognized this as the Mississippi, yet a curious thing now transpired. In that familiar manner he raised his head and sniffed, but his nose was turned toward the east rather than the north, and in a moment he padded off in that direction, away from the river.

This was a country dotted with lakes of various sizes and shapes, a country just beginning to come alive with the first touches of new growth. Buds on the hardwoods had begun to swell, and in clear spaces between the pine forests there were stretches of ground which took on a distinctly pale greenish hue when seen from a distance, as new grasses sprouted and old blades regained some color.

He traveled through these dense forests of pine and cedar and reveled in the sweet fresh aroma of their needles. He encountered creatures he had not seen before and reacted warily to most of them. A large, lumbering black bear, freshly out of hibernation, caused him to halt in his tracks when they were still fifty feet apart. For ten minutes he watched as the large animal tore bark from standing dead trees and old logs lying on the ground, seeking dormant insect grubs. But then the bear saw him, raised his nose with a curious snuffling sound and began ambling in his direction. At once the crossbreed sped away.

Another time, while chasing a snowshoe rabbit, whose fur was in a mottled stage as it changed from winter white to summer brown, he raced around a craggy bluff and very nearly collided with a large gray wolf. Without a moment's hesitation he sprinted for the nearest tree, a lofty pine, with the wolf close behind. His bad foot seemed to hamper him not at all as he raced up the rough trunk, nor did he stop until well over half the tree was below him.

The wolf circled the tree a few times and once stood on his hind legs with his front paws braced against the trunk, staring up at the crossbreed. But he was really not very interested and soon loped carelessly away.

For over an hour the crossbreed remained where he was, and just as he began descending, he saw a movement on a branch not far below his own, but halfway around the tree. Perched there was a rather large animal watching him calmly but steadily. It was about the size of a raccoon, but strangely different in appearance. At once curious, the crossbreed moved to get a closer look.

He returned to the trunk of the tree, went down a few feet and stepped onto the thick branch supporting this queer animal. As he did so, the creature turned around so that its backside was toward the intruder and its short tail rested on the branch. It hunched itself distinctly and suddenly seemed larger as its dark fur, intermingled with what appeared to be thick white hairs, stood out from its body.

The crossbreed had never encountered a porcupine before, and so, though alive with curiosity, he approached cautiously. Once before a black-and-white animal had caused him grief. This animal made no move to get farther away, and so, when the crossbreed came up to only a foot behind it, he stopped. He cocked his head to one side, studied the creature and then hesitantly extended a paw to touch it.

Just as he did so, the porcupine swept its tail in a quick arc. The tail missed striking the crossbreed's paw, but despite the speed with which the cat jerked back, it still barely nicked his foreleg. At once there was a stinging pain as two small quills stabbed deeply and stuck to him. Again the porcupine swung its tail, but by this time the crossbreed was already scrambling down the tree almost as swiftly as he had scaled it.

He leaped the last fifteen feet to the ground and ran fifty yards or more before stopping. The three-inch quills were painful, sticking in the flesh just above the wrist of his foreleg, and they seemed to dig in more deeply with every move he made. For a long time he worked at them, biting at their ends and tugging to pull them free. It was not easy to do. Not only were the quills extremely pointed, but just a fraction of an inch below the tip of each there were numerous microscopic barbs. These barbs had begun to spread as soon as they encountered the body heat of the crossbreed.

He got them out at last, though not without considerable effort and pain, nor without tearing his own flesh in the process. He licked the wounds thoroughly, cast a final glance at the tree he had left and then trotted off, stepping carefully around the two quills on the ground and once again limping slightly.

Though the encounter was unfortunate for him, it could have been a great deal worse, perhaps even fatal. More than one predator has died as the result of being slapped in the face or mouth by a porcupine's tail, and such a death was usually a long and painful one: not caused by the quills themselves, for they were not venomous, but because the victim could not dislodge them from snout, lips and tongue. The wounds would fester and swell and, unable to eat or perhaps even to drink, the predator must soon die of hunger or thirst.

This injury for the crossbreed, however, was not serious. Within a few days it had ceased to bother him, and he no longer favored that leg. Again he had learned a lesson that might prevent a fatal misjudgment at some later date. He continued his journey.

It was on the day he reached the Snake River, midway between the towns of Brunswick and Grasston, however, that his progress was unexpectedly halted. A short while before he reached that stream a raging thunderstorm had overtaken him and he had sought shelter in a hollow log. He trembled and moaned when lightning slashed through the skies and struck with earth-jarring cracks here and there around him. Once a huge pine, no more than sixty yards from him, was virtually disintegrated and crashed to earth in a smoking pile. Rain fell in torrents, extinguishing the smoldering embers and then, nearly as swiftly as it had come, the storm was past. Along the western horizon a trace of blue sky showed through the clouds, and hardly half an hour later, the atmosphere was clear and bright, and sunlight sparkled off a multitude of droplets everywhere.

Resuming his travel, the crossbreed soon found his path barred by the roily, tumbling waters of the Snake River. He followed it downstream for an hour, staying close to shore. When he came to where another huge tree had been shattered by the lightning and lay across his path, he began to detour around it.

That was when he heard the faint cry.

He stopped and turned his head, his ears twitching in order to locate the sound. The little cry came again, and now he had it pinpointed. Slowly, his senses keenly alert, he approached the splintered bole. There, wandering dazedly in front of it, was a tiny kitten, a female who was probably not much older than the crossbreed himself had been when the great storm-caused flood had permanently altered his own life.

The crossbreed's tail twitched and a deep soft whine left him, but the kitten had not seen him and apparently did not hear the sound. Again the crossbreed cried out, this time with a clearly audible yowl. Strangely, the little female still paid no attention.

Very curious now, the crossbreed glanced about him, but could see no other living thing. He trotted up to the kitten which, at the moment, was reaching out her paw to tentatively touch a small pine cone. Even though the crossbreed made no effort to approach silently, she obviously did not hear him, and when he touched his nose to her backside, she jumped as if shot and landed with her feet widespread, her back arched and a frightened hissing issuing from her mouth.

Then, with a plaintive little cry, she abruptly ran to him and rubbed against his legs. Almost at once she began purring, and when the crossbreed merely stood there looking bewildered, she licked his leg and then lay down directly between his front feet.

Seemingly taken aback, the crossbreed stepped away a foot or so, and the two animals stared at one another. In a nearby bush a bluejay screamed raucously, and automatically the crossbreed's ears twitched toward the sound. The kitten never moved a whisker.

She was deaf.

A slight shift of the wind brought a new scent to the crossbreed, and now, his hackles slightly raised, he moved toward the shattered bole of the tree and peered inside. The kitten waddled awkwardly behind him and bumped clumsily into his hind legs when he stopped. Even as he looked, his hackles lowered. Inside the hollow bole of the shattered stump section lay the crushed remains of a large female lynx and two other kittens.

It was not difficult to reconstruct what had happened: its trunk instantaneously shattered by the lightning bolt, the upper part of this tree had simply dropped a few feet into its own hollow bole before toppling over. And in this bole had been the lynx and her three kittens. The wonder of it all was how the little female, rubbing against the crossbreed's hind legs right now, had escaped the fate that had smitten the rest of her family.

The mother lynx had apparently been not much heavier than the crossbreed, although the length of her legs indicated she had stood considerably higher. What fur remained that was not crushed or discolored with blood was much lighter than his own, a faint grayish tan mottled with dark brown spots. Her feet were unusually large and her tail black-tipped and even shorter than his. The tufts on her cheeks and ears were much more pronounced.

Instinctively the crossbreed backed away from the tree, bowling over the female kitten as he did so. Apparently she thought he was playing with her, for she bounded a few comical steps away and laid her forepaws and chin on the ground, while her rump stuck up in the air and the tiny stub of tail jiggled excitedly back and forth.

The crossbreed disregarded her and began walking away, but immediately she followed him. He stopped and turned his head and snarled lightly at her, but the sound didn't penetrate and the bared teeth did not frighten her.

Suddenly he turned and loped away into some thick brush. At the end of fifty feet he stopped and listened. The kitten was following, obviously having a most difficult time pushing her way through the heavier material and now wailing piteously. For a moment it appeared the crossbreed would move on, but then he returned to the little female and leaned his muzzle close to her. The mewing was replaced at once by a barely audible purring as she rubbed her back against his head.

Hesitantly at first, but then with greater assurance, the crossbreed licked her, and now, for the first time in more than a year, his own chest vibrated with a deep rumbling purr.

XVIII

Less than a mile farther down the Snake River from where he had discovered the kitten—a journey which had taken them almost four hours—the crossbreed found a roomy abandoned den at the base of a great rock jutting from the forest floor. He hid the kitten carefully in some dense brush nearby, nosing her to the ground until she seemed to understand he meant for her to stay there. Then he warily inspected the den.

His sensitive nose told him that a bear had been here for some time, but that it was gone now and had not been back for many days. The hole had obviously been used only for hibernation and not as a permanent lair. Other than the fleeting scent of a chipmunk, no other animal odor could be detected. Satisfied, the crossbreed trotted back to the kitten, picked her up by the scruff and, holding her high, carried her into the den.

Her fur was bespattered with mud from their passage, and so now he cleansed her quite thoroughly with his tongue. She made the job a bit more difficult by batting at his bobbing nose with her forepaws but he didn't appear to mind. He stayed with her until dusk when, thoroughly worn out from her long walk and boisterous play, the kitten dropped off into a deep slumber, her body leaning against him.

En route to this new home, the crossbreed had caught three mice and had torn them apart for the kitten. That she had been partially or wholly weaned was evident from the gusto with which she attacked this fresh meat, gobbling hungrily and without pause. He had given all of it to her and so now, hungry himself, he got to his feet and left the den. The kitten did not even awaken.

Hunting was better than usual. Apparently the rabbits and mice were eager to be out of their soggy hiding places and to run about. Almost within sight of the rocky den he caught the scent of a rabbit and crouched. A cottontail was hopping along determinedly in his direction. Not until it was six feet away did it sense the cat's presence. By then it was too late. Though it sprang to one side, the crossbreed caught it in four bounds and nailed it to the ground with his own weight while his teeth bit deeply. The rabbit stiffened and died.

He crouched on the spot, ate it all and then continued his ranging. In a nearby area of last summer's dried goose grass he successively caught and ate three meadow voles. Then, even though his hunger was largely appeased, he continued his hunt.

Less than an hour later, not more than a mile from the town of Brunswick, he once again caught the scent of a rabbit and crouched very low to the ground. Though he had not seen his intended prey, he stayed downwind and followed the scent, moving with extreme care and silence. Step by slow step, his body stretched out amazingly behind him, he moved ever closer and then he saw her.

The big female snowshoe rabbit was crouched over a small depression in the ground where her family of five little fawns were reaching up to nurse from her. She was only eight feet from him now and, with no other cover to hide him and her discovery of him imminent, he dashed out at her. So unexpected was his attack that, even though the doe leaped at once, he caught her within a foot of the nest and snapped her neck with a single savage bite.

The fawns were scattering frantically through the grasses. He dropped her and quickly caught and killed one of the young. He ate it at once and then, no longer in the least hungry, he picked up the flaccid form of the big rabbit in his mouth and headed for the den.

The kitten was still sleeping when he returned to the den, and he dropped the rabbit a couple of feet away and lay down beside her. She partially wakened when he licked her a few times, but then she wriggled closer to his side and promptly went back to sleep.

Spring and summer passed swiftly for the strange pair and, especially during those first few weeks, it was a busy time for the crossbreed. It was also a peculiarly gratifying time for him. For the first time in his life another creature was dependent upon him, and he actually seemed to revel in the fact, undertaking the raising of this adopted kitten with every bit as much devotion and protectiveness as if she were his own offspring. He hunted well for her, and not once did she go hungry, nor did he.

In a very short time indeed, he was teaching her the fundamentals of hunting, but having an inordinately difficult time in doing so; not because he was a poor teacher, but because his student was totally deaf—undoubtedly the result of the frightening blast of lightning that had taken the lives of her family.

Her very deafness, however, seemed to sharpen her senses of sight and smell. She learned to lie facing downwind so that, if an enemy approached unseen and unheard behind her, she would detect his scent and be prepared. And, above all, she watched her crossbreed teacher carefully, and even though the low sounds he made did not register with her, she grew to understand through his actions what was expected of her.

The lack of continuous cross-country traveling and having someone to provide for had been good for the crossbreed, too. By early autumn he had not only gained back the weight he had lost, but more besides, and he was in excellent physical condition.

The little lynx grew rapidly and by late October was a bit taller than he, though still not nearly as heavy. She was delicately boned and a beautiful creature, her coat a light fawn color speckled with rich brown spots. Her four-inch black-tipped tail was two inches shorter than the crossbreed's, but her cheek and ear tufts, like her mother's, were much more prominent than his. Her forehead, brows and cheek tufts were streaked with deep brown, and the muttonchop appearance of the cheeks imparted a ludicrously sober look to her expression. Her feet were easily half again as broad as the crossbreed's, and her eyes were a deep, clear yellow-orange.

For more than half a year they had been inseparable, and not once during this time had the strange urge struck the crossbreed to raise his head in that peculiar manner and sniff the air for some vague and elusive scent. It almost seemed that in the young female he had found what had so relentlessly driven him on.

Such, however, was not the case.

On the fifth day of November, as they ranged near the mouth of the Snake River where it empties into the St. Croix River, the young female went into heat for the first time. Overnight the relationship between them changed drastically. The crossbreed's interest ceased being paternal and, instead, became sexual. She did not fight him off, but what she did do was even worse; she ignored him. Everywhere she went, he followed her closely, and only when he came too near to her did she strike out at him, not in the manner of a female cat fighting her lover, but rather in the nature of one animal warning another to stay away or suffer the consequences.

He did not understand and could only continue to dog her every step and accept with apparently hurt confusion the lashing of her fully bared claws at him and the teeth which bit rather than nipped playfully. This standoff lasted for three days, during which time the crossbreed slept little, drank little and ate not at all—a regimen not calculated to improve his temperament.

Then a large male lynx appeared. One minute the crossbreed and the female were standing ten or twelve feet apart in a little copse of the forest only a dozen yards from the St. Croix River, and the next minute the strange cat was on the scene. Neither of them had heard or sensed his approach.

He was larger by far than either of them, fully eighteen inches tall at the shoulder and no less than forty pounds. He was a proud, handsome animal with extremely peaked black-tipped ears and great flaring cheek tufts. His coloration was even lighter than that of the female, and it was immediately obvious that he meant to have her.

If he was startled to find this female—whose heat scent he had detected from several miles away and followed here—in the company of a cat not of her own species, he showed no indication of it. He walked into the clearing from the screen of underbrush in an exaggeratedly stiff-legged fashion, his ears flat against his head and a powerful growl rumbling deep in his chest.

Perhaps he anticipated that his size and menacing nature would cow and discourage the smaller suitor, but if so, he had underestimated the crossbreed. He had taken no more than four steps toward the female, who had begun to crouch and whine in the traditional manner of courtship, when the crossbreed attacked.

The reflexes of the lynx were every bit as quick as those of the crossbreed. He was a much older and more experienced animal and he met the attack with a leap of his own. The pair clinched, biting and clawing at one another, a frenzied caterwauling erupting from both. Bits of fur wafted out and away from them, and soon bright red flecks of blood began staining their underbellies and flanks.

One of them—it was difficult to say which—shrieked in anguish as his opponent found an opening for strong teeth, but the sound degenerated to one of snarling anger and the battle continued. For the first five minutes or so, they seemed evenly matched, but then the greater size, weight and experience of the lynx began to tell.

The crossbreed was forced back farther and farther toward the river until they were battling on the very shoreline. Another anguished screech came, and this time there could be no doubt that it had come from him. The side of his face had been laid open by the murderous claws of the lynx, and an instant later the jaws tore a ragged rent in the flesh of his right hip.

Perhaps even then he might have found a momentary opening in his opponent's defenses and regained the upper hand, but unexpectedly there was a blur of grayish-tan fur and the adopted female slammed into his side, biting and clawing him in a frenzy.

Stunned not only by the physical impact and the shocking breach of courtship battle behavior, but equally by the fact that his own adopted offspring should attack him, the crossbreed faltered. In that instant the lynx had him by the throat, knocked him onto his back on the gravel and was astraddle him. A yard away from them the female poised in a half-crouch, her own ears tight against her head, her eyes squinted to the barest slits and a murderous snarl in her throat.

The lynx heard her, too, and for just an instant he relaxed his own hold in order to shift his head so he could better watch her. It was an opportunity the crossbreed did not let pass. With a tremendous exertion he drew his hind feet up and slammed the exposed claws down the length of his adversary's stomach, at the same time twisting out of the grasp on his own throat.

The lynx screeched as if scalded and jerked back. It was the break the crossbreed needed. With a tremendous bound he sailed outward a dozen feet or more before splashing into the water and, the instant he hit, his legs were churning to carry him to the other side. The lynx ran into the water up to his knees and stood there momentarily undecided. Abruptly he shook himself and turned back to the dainty female who was crouching, awaiting his approach and snarling with something akin to coyness. She never even glanced at her fleeing benefactor.

The crossbreed, for the third time in his life, found himself on his own on a powerful river. The water was frigid and he swam with an urgency born of the knowledge that he could not last long in such numbing cold. The St. Croix was easily fifty yards wide at this point and its current was very strong. His speed downstream was greater by far than his speed cross-stream. When at last he felt the gravel of the opposite shallows under his feet and staggered stiffly out of the icy water, he was far below the point where he had entered it.

With the temperature close to freezing, he knew better than just to stand still or walk slowly. Trembling badly, he shook himself to rid his fur of much of the water clinging to it. His body ached, the rips in his hide hurt and his muscles seemed to respond reluctantly, sluggishly, to the demands he made of them.

He glanced briefly upstream and diagonally across the river, but saw no sign of either of the lynxes. In a moment he turned back, and for the first time in months lifted his head in that peculiar gesture that had become so characteristic of him. The compulsive yearning had returned, stronger than ever. He shook himself again and set off at an easy run along this Wisconsin shore of the St. Croix River.

This time he was heading due south.

XIX

Though he continued his southerly course, the cross-breed traveled rather slowly. Often, if hunting was good, he stayed for many days in one particular location. He followed the St. Croix River downstream, giving wide berth to the little villages of Randall and Wolfcreek.

Four or five miles north of the city of St. Croix Falls, he came to a highway which paralleled the river, and the nearer he came to the large town, the more traffic swept by on the road. Recognizing that it would be dangerous for him to get any closer to the heavily populated area, he crossed the highway and began moving in a southeasterly direction.

There were many small frozen lakes in this countryside and an abundance of mice and rabbits. Along the banks of the Apple River five or six miles north of the town of Star Prairie, he found an ideal unoccupied den, where he took up a semipermanent residency for nearly two months.

It was by far the best den he had ever had: a natural little cave which opened from a steep bank overlooking Apple River, its mouth well hidden by a screen of brush, vines and saplings. It ran back into the hillside almost twenty yards before suddenly ending in a little domed room, roughly circular and perhaps five feet in diameter. That at least one bobcat or lynx had used it as a den before him was evident from the scattering of small bones pushed to one side, but so long ago had the residency been that no trace of the scent of the other animal remained.

While he often ranged far from this den and not infrequently even spent a night or two away from it, he still used it as his prime base of operations. If his kill of prey was made relatively near to the den, he would carry it back there and eat it at his leisure. When far from his den, he wolfed it down without lost time. And it was not unusual for him to range as much as forty or fifty miles away.

Prey—especially snowshoe rabbits—seemed most plentiful along the shores of the creeks, rivers and lakes, and so he prowled along their edges extensively. He quickly came to know very well the shorelines of the lakes closest to him, lakes with names indicative of their characteristics: Sand Lake and Long Lake, Island, Pine, Big and Mud Lakes, Deer, Cedar and Oakridge lakes. But though he learned their shorelines well, he knew even better the courses of the streams within his range and he hunted along them for considerable distances.

More than once he followed the Apple River downstream the thirty-five miles or so to its mouth on the St. Croix and even down that larger river some distance. The Willow and Kinnickinnic rivers he followed until their valleys became too populated near the towns of Hudson—also on the St. Croix—and River Falls, which was only fifteen miles from where the St. Croix joined the Mississippi.

Twice during those weeks he roamed south until he hit the headwaters of the Rush River. The first time he followed it downstream only as far as the town of Martel and then swung in a wide semicircle to the east, hit the South Fork of Hay River and followed it back upstream until it petered out about ten miles from his den. The second and last time he followed Rush River downstream was in mid-February. He had no inkling, when he began his ranging this time, that he would not again return to the Apple River den.

He was in superb physical condition now. Though bearing a few scars from his fight with the lynx, he had suffered no permanent damage, and the wounds had quickly healed. Not once in these weeks had he been forced to go hungry, and his wide ranging hardened his muscles, quickened his reflexes and sharpened his mind. On the day he left his den for the last time, he was just short of sixteen inches tall at the shoulder and weighed exactly thirty-eight pounds.

He skirted widely the river-intersected towns of New Centerville, Martel and El Paso as he traveled along the east bank of the Rush River, and on the third night, again reached the Mississippi River at the upper portion of that extremely wide stretch known as Lake Pepin. Here he angled eastward, away from the river, and met Plum Creek just to the south of Plum City. He turned to the north, apparently to follow this smaller creek to its source and then return to his den, but abruptly he stopped and turned around, sniffing the air carefully.

At once he stepped out onto the ice and walked to the five-foot gap of still-running water in the center of the creek and leaped effortlessly to the other side. He trotted downstream a few hundred yards and then climbed the bank and moved off diagonally to the southeast. The scent became stronger, and an anxious whine filled his throat at intervals.

It was yet an hour until dawn when he crossed a roughly paved secondary road only a few hundred yards outside the darkened village of Porcupine and headed for a large woods not far south of it. Just as certainly as if he had already seen her, he knew that there he would find a female bobcat in the height of heat, and now he broke into a smooth run, his whining louder and more eager.

He raced through the woods a quarter of a mile until

abruptly bursting into the clearing where she crouched snarling, her eyes fixed on the large male bobcat similarly poised a few yards in front of her. Both of them turned their heads to eye the newcomer, and at once a menacing growl came from the male.

Without pause, the crossbreed raced across the clearing and flung himself bodily at the bobcat, who rose on his hind legs to meet him. The bobcat was slightly the smaller and undoubtedly the younger of the two, and against the near forty pounds of fury enclosed within the hide of the crossbreed he didn't fare too well. The fight was brief and savage. The pair rolled about in the clearing, a shrieking tangle of claws and teeth and flying fur. Within minutes, the bobcat broke away with a frenzied yowling and sprinted off into the woods.

For perhaps twenty yards the crossbreed followed him, but then, satisfied he would not return, went back to the female. She was sitting alertly, eyes wide and ears erect, where she had been when the conflict broke out. But as soon as the crossbreed trotted toward her, she flattened her ears, crouched and hissed. Undaunted, he pounced upon her and they, too, rolled about in the clearing, their weird screams in the new light of dawn frightening and eerie.

Six different times they fought briefly and broke apart before she suddenly sprang away as fast as she could run. It was part of the game, and in an instant the crossbreed was pursuing and gradually closing the gap.

She was an excellent runner. Twice when he had pulled up to within a foot of her, she dodged expertly and opened the gap again considerably before he could follow. They raced across a small highway which ran the eleven miles between Pepin and Ella, and the crossbreed narrowly missed being struck by a silver tank truck, filled with milk, which was rumbling toward Pepin. He hardly even noticed.

They raced into an extensive woods and then into a prairie beyond it through which a small creek meandered, one of its banks much higher and steeper than the other. And finally, close to where a tremendous granite boulder jutted from the upper bank, he caught her and rolled over with her, and then they lay side by side for several minutes panting heavily.

She rubbed her head against his chin and licked his feet, forelegs and cheek tufts. He responded by licking her face and ears, and the deep rumbling purr from both of them was clearly audible several feet away. They mated then and he bit her back and neck and shoulders gently, while a penetrating, rather melodious whining cry came from the female.

Later, when they stood together and walked alongside one another to the top of the high bank a few feet from the boulder, the female continued walking along the rim; but the crossbreed suddenly stopped and she went on, ten or twelve feet, before halting to look back at him curiously.

For the moment the crossbreed had no eyes for her. There was something so strangely familiar about this area: the rocky creekbed with its trickling flow of water, one bank high and the other low, the point of woodland stretching into the prairie from upstream and, most of all, this enormous, round granite boulder thrusting up from the soil. Abruptly he recognized these surroundings, and an odd, plaintive, almost inaudible cry escaped him.

This was where he had been born.

There, upstream a short distance, was where his sire had plunged along, dragging the trap that held his foot, where the branch to which the trap had been attached had become wedged, where he was ultimately clubbed to death. There, diagonally across the creek, fifty feet or so from him, was where the log had rested in which he had been born and in which he had taken that perilous journey on the crest of the flood that had wiped out his family. And here, beside him at this moment, was the very rock he had known so well and had looked upon so often from the hollow stub of branch projecting from that log. After a passage of over twenty-two hundred miles and almost exactly four years, he had returned to his birthplace.

Despite that devastating flood, the area had not changed very much. The banks were subtly different and in one or two places the flow of the creek had altered slightly, but mostly it was pretty much the same. And now, as he had been doing off and on for so long, he raised his head, listened and sniffed and looked for something unheard, unscented, unseen.

Apparently mystified at the action of her mate, the female came back to him and rubbed against his side. When still he didn't respond to her, she began to walk around behind him. Suddenly she gave a queer, strangled grunt, leaped high into the air and flopped to the ground kicking. At the same instant a terrible, burning blow struck the rear end of the crossbreed and spun him halfway around. Even as the female was still in the air, the sound of the shot came, a heavy, reverberating crack. A moment later another bullet barely skimmed through the hairs on the crossbreed's back without touching his skin and struck the big boulder, ricocheting away with a fearsome scream. Again, following it, came the sound of the shot.

The crossbreed scrambled over the edge of the bank and half fell into the shallow creek below. His tail had been short before—no more than six inches long—but it was now considerably shorter. The bullet, which had slammed into his mate, had first ripped through his tail less than two inches from his rump, severing bone and flesh, until it hung by only a few gristly strands. As he galloped down the rocky creekbed, droplets of blood spattered his hindquarters.

He remained in the creekbed for a quarter mile and left it only as it skirted a large wooded area. He plunged into the heavier cover and continued to run in a wide half-circle. When he came to the edge of the woods again, four hundred yards or more from where he had entered, he stopped and peered out with extreme caution.

A lone man carrying a heavy rifle was just approaching the big rock. He stopped on the edge of the high bank and looked upstream and downstream, then all around him carefully. He stuck out his booted foot then and nudged the still form of the bobcat. A moment later he picked the animal up by one hind foot and slung her over his shoulder. Then he began following the creek downstream.

At once the crossbreed turned and ran deeper into the woods, worming his way through the heaviest brush. As he plunged through a great thicket of briers, the dangling section of his tail caught and pulled away. He ran on without even appearing to notice the loss. Half an hour later he emerged from the woods several miles to the south and stood there trembling slightly as he looked at the broad, ice-rimmed expanse of the Chippewa River flowing past at his feet.

For ten minutes he stood there motionless, his head slightly raised and only his nostrils barely twitching as he tested the air. At length he dropped to his stomach and for as many minutes longer bent his head far back and licked the small stump of tail.

Then with no display of grief for his missing mate and evidently not in any great deal of pain from the injury, he set off at an easy trot downstream along the shoreline of the Chippewa.

He followed this northwest bank of the river to its mouth on the Mississippi, passing only one bridge en route, about a mile and a half above the greater river. When he discovered that there was no way for him to cross the Chippewa at its mouth, he paused uncertainly and once again performed his strange sniffing ritual. Then he doubled back roughly in the direction whence he had come, though this time angling away from the river slightly.

The last food he had eaten was a pair of deer mice some four hours earlier, and he was very hungry. When he caught the scent of a rabbit, perhaps a quarter mile from the river, he followed it up until the cottontail burst from cover and set off in a desperate run. The crossbreed pursued, and though the rabbit maneuvered wildly and twice dodged the big cat just at the last possible moment, eventually he pounced upon it and the life of the rodent ended in a shrill squealing.

Close by, hidden from view by a heavy screen of brush, was the highway which crossed the Chippewa not far from here. Even while the crossbreed tore the rabbit apart and devoured it, he heard several cars hiss past. When he had finished, he remained where he was for a considerable while, again licking the stump of his tail, but now whining faintly with the pain. The wound was hurting considerably more than when the bullet had first severed the tail, and when he regained his feet and began to walk, it was with pronounced stiffness.

He traveled alongside the highway, though hidden from it, until once again he reached the bridge he had passed earlier. The sun had now been up for a couple of hours and, while traffic on the road was not actually heavy, it would have been most dangerous for him to attempt a crossing of the span.

Instead, he went underneath it and padded, unseen, to the other side of the highway where he broke into a rather awkward lope until he reached the woodland beyond. Keeping within a mile of the bridge, he circled about until he found where a long, downed V-shaped tree trunk lay, the top of the V partially screened over by viny material. Into this hiding place he moved, settled himself as comfortably as possible and, well hidden, immediately went to sleep.

Throughout the day as he slept, an occasional, faint whimpering sound left him, and his feet twitched. It was the exact same sound he made at those times when he would raise his head and sniff for the scent which always seemed to elude him.

The Cross...

XX

It was an hour or more after darkness had fallen when the crossbreed left his place of concealment. He moved on a direct line back to the Chippewa River and followed it to the bridge. He approached the structure with great caution. In the deep shadow of an abutment he stood and listened for a long while.

Only one car passed, and a minute after it was out of his hearing the crossbreed ran up the embankment and did not slacken his pace until he had crossed the bridge, raced down the northeast embankment and reached the nearby woods. Then he slowed to the usual loping pace he maintained when ranging. His injured tail still hurt him, but it no longer hampered his movements.

He was actively hunting again but, more than that, he was moving on a very determined course in a wide arc. He crossed a small highway just south of Mishi Mokwa and continued his curving route until, a short time after midnight, he intersected the little Buffalo River just below the town of Modena. Here he turned and followed the small stream downriver. Within four miles he had caught and eaten a half-dozen meadow voles and deer mice in a prairie which was pleasantly abundant with the little rodents.

In this same field he stopped and then began to wind his way sinuously through the thick, dry grass toward the strong scent that had just reached him. Though the grass was old and brown and very thick, hardly a whisper of sound heralded his passage, and within sixty feet he had approached to within striking distance.

Not until he was in the air in his final swift pounce did the hen pheasant realize she was in danger. With a startled cry she leaped up, wings flailing, but the crossbreed had her before she had more than just cleared the grasses. He pulled her back to the ground with him and rolled over with her, and when they stopped, she was dead, her head lolling on its broken neck.

The crossbreed ate almost all of her, attacking first the plump breast and vital organs and then finishing with the thighs and lower legs. He was pleasantly full when he was through and he cleaned himself thoroughly before resuming his passage.

Another mile or so downstream he came to where a country road bridged the little Buffalo River. There were no houses nearby here and he trotted across the span rather nonchalantly, even pausing in the center to raise his head and briefly sniff. On the other side of the bridge he struck out just a little west of due south, but moving considerably slower.

An hour before dawn, as he walked through a wooded area, he encountered a little creek barely five feet across and began following it downstream. Twice in the next few minutes he stopped to sniff and cocked his head, listening. In quick succession he passed the points where a few other similarly sized tributaries entered and the creek became deeper and wider. When he came to where a fallen tree formed a little natural bridge across the stream, he stood looking at it for a long moment before resuming his walk.

He moved in a peculiar manner now, stiffly and rather awkwardly, head almost constantly held very high and nose slightly uplifted. He seemed unusually

intent, and every dozen feet or so he paused and stood quietly with his ears twitching slightly. And then, as he rounded a screen of brush, he jarred to a halt and a sudden trembling wracked him. On the opposite shore, half collapsed into the water of the creek, was what remained of a little wooden pier—a pier he had once known very well. Beyond the pier a small path wound through the brush and then angled up the steep bank.

A long, moaning cry escaped him and carried eerily through the new dawn. Three times more he cried out in this same manner as the trembling continued to ripple over his entire body.

He turned then and ran rapidly back to where the fallen tree leaned across the creek, and without hesitation he raced over it. Once before he had run across this very tree. On the opposite side he ran up the bank and didn't stop until he had reached the edge of the woods where a long, sloping prairie began. This was *his* prairie, where he and the boy had roamed together. This was the prairie where they had hunted mice together and where he had pounced upon and devoured his first warm-blooded prey—four nestling meadowlarks. And there, at the far upper end of the prairie, was an old, ramshackle frame house, and beside the house a short distance away was a shed.

His shed.

Again the deep moaning sound came from him, growing in volume until it was a far-carrying yowl. Even as the excited sound continued coming from him, he raced across the prairie toward the house and shed, and not until he was only forty yards from them did he suddenly stop and sink to the grass until he was all but hidden. It was as if suddenly he had remembered that here, too, was where he had been shot at for the first time in his life.

Now he moved toward the yard slowly, cautiously, every sense intensely alert. When he was still twenty yards from the house he heard a car coming down the old rutted road in this direction. Automatically he did as he had done dozens of other times when cars came toward him: he flattened himself in the dense weeds until he was well hidden and waited for the car to pass.

This car didn't pass. There was no place for it to go; the old house was at the end of the road. The car, a heavily loaded station wagon with windows badly fogged, entered the yard, turned in a circle and stopped with its motor still idling.

Now there was nowhere for the crossbreed to go. The woods were much too far away for him to leap up and dash away in an effort to reach them safely, nor did he dare to try to race out of sight around the house or shed. He had no choice but to hold the position he was in and perhaps avoid detection, but ready to fight or flee in an instant if threatened.

A deep, quiet growl rumbled in the crossbreed's chest, and his lip curled in a vicious snarl.

XXI

The station wagon was so loaded that even though there were only two occupants, they were virtually wedged into place in their seats. They had left Alma at dawn and would probably still be riding at sunset, since it was nearly five hundred miles to St. Louis and some of the roads were apt to be icy.

As they had come to the old cutoff from the main highway a few miles below Alma, Maude Andrews slowed and then had carefully turned and maneuvered past the sawhorse barricade and onto the badly pitted old road. She wished now she hadn't promised Todd they'd stop by their old place for "one last look." She had no desire to see it again, and though she knew Todd had pedaled down here on his bicycle numerous times, she had never come back to the old house herself since they had left it several years ago.

She turned her head and studied her son, unable to understand what attraction this place could have for him. It had never been much of a home; not for him, not for any of them. Nothing had ever pleased her quite so much as when they had left it to move into nearby Alma. The house in town hadn't been much in itself, of course, but it was infinitely better than this one they had left. Old man Scanlon, who owned it, hadn't even been able to rent it again—little wonder!—and according to Todd the place had just fallen apart.

Todd didn't realize his mother was looking at him. He was lost in his own thoughts. At sixteen, his clothing was all too small, even though relatively new, and his voice cracked badly when he spoke. He was very conscious of this and embarrassed by it, and as a result he didn't talk a great deal.

Now, as they bumped along this last rutted mile to the old place, he thought about his lost pet. Time after time he'd come back here on his bicycle and roamed about in the areas where he and the kitten had roamed. He had walked through the woods and prairie where they had ambled together and he had gone by the little dock, now all caved in and useless, and he had sat in solitude inside the little shed and dreamed and hoped.

For almost two years he had half expected to find his beloved pet had come home and, each time he arrived, he would cup his mouth and loudly call "Yowler! Yowler!" But there had never been an answering yowl, and he was certain now that there would never be. Nevertheless, he wanted this last lingering look.

They pulled into the yard, turned around and stopped beside the rusting hulk of their old car. Neither of them spoke. Todd's eyes were fixed on the house but his thoughts were years away.

He remembered the joyful times when he and the kitten had gone fishing together in the little rowboat and how they'd hunted mice in the prairie. He remembered the first time he brought the half-drowned kitten to the pier and he recalled equally well the spot across the creek from it where he'd found Yowler that last day, after Paw had shot at him.

He relived briefly their flight downriver together and how he had fallen in and been marooned on the island while the boat had drifted away in the current; and the miserable night he had spent after that, hunched in his wet clothes beside the fire he had built, thankful for the fact that the canvas pack with the matches in it had landed on the shore when he fell in, but thoroughly disgusted with himself for his clumsiness.

And what had happened to the boat? Had it finally drifted ashore somewhere and the young cat escaped? Or had someone shot the animal when they saw him drifting along in the boat? Or had he fallen out and drowned? A hundred times and more he had asked himself these questions during that long night and since.

Early the next morning an outboard motorboat had come skimming to the island, his fire having been seen by a resident high on the hills across the river during the night, and he had been rescued and returned home to a frantic mother and deeply worried father. It had been a bad time for all of them, but just as his mother had so often told him, it was always darkest before the dawn and somehow, from that time on, things had seemed to get better—except that his pet was gone. Paw had gotten another job, this time in La Crosse and, surprisingly, he had stayed with it. He still drank some, but not like before. It was as if he had been shocked into trying harder to be a better husband and a better father.

Then, the next summer, Paw's brother James—Uncle Jimmy—had died and left all his worldly goods, which amounted to a little service station in Alma, to Paw. Paw had done well with it, too, and the working for himself instead of for someone else seemed to be the inspiration he had needed to make good. Recently he had sold that station, and now he was down in St. Louis at the new and better one he'd bought a partnership in and he was doing very well. It was a new life and a better one for them all, and Todd was glad they were going to the city. Yet, there remained a deep nostalgia in him for this place.

He was suddenly jarred out of his reverie by the touch of his mother's hand on his arm. He looked over at her and smiled faintly.

"Ready, Toddy?" she asked softly.

He nodded. "Ready, Maw. I don't think I ever want to come back here again."

She flashed an understanding smile at him, patted his cheek and then put the car in gear and started back down the rutted lane toward the highway. Neither she nor her son saw the large feline head rise up from the weeds.

All the while the station wagon had parked there, the crossbreed had remained still. He did not understand it, or even attempt to understand, when no one got out of the car, nor did he know why, just as suddenly as it had come, the car had pulled away.

He raised his head slightly above the dead grasses and watched the vehicle bump out of sight down the dirt road, and for another five minutes after that he remained where he was. At last he stood and looked at the old house.

There was no sign of life in or around it. Though the temperature hovered near freezing, no wisp of smoke drifted up from the chimney and, in fact, several of the windows were missing and the door was open and hanging by only one hinge at the bottom.

As if recognizing that he now had nothing to fear, the crossbreed paced boldly to the buildings. The junked car was there beside the house, its hood missing and wheels gone, its windows shattered. The cat walked entirely around the house and caught neither scent nor sound of any human. Hesitantly he stepped onto the sagging porch and even more hesitantly stuck his head in the open doorway.

Nothing. No scent of humans; no furnishings; no trace of habitation; nothing except a little mouse which scurried from under a piece of cardboard and vanished into a crack in the floor. The crossbreed wasn't interested in it.

He turned and left the porch and walked to the shed and circled it. The window he used to enter and leave by now had a large, battered piece of tin—an old softdrink sign—nailed to it and the keg that had sat

beneath the windowsill was gone. Except for a gap of
about an inch, the door was closed, and when he
touched his nose to it, it swung open a foot or more
before bumping against something.

He stuck his head in and again there was no human
scent; only a vague smell of the mice that regularly
prowled about the interior. He entered and stood in the
middle of the floor, looking about him. Some of the old
boxes were gone and others were shifted, but it was
essentially the same. Beneath the tin-sealed window,
several of its panes broken away, was the cardboard
soup-can carton in which he had spent so much of his
kittenhood, and he walked to it now and sniffed at it.
Inside were the feed bags upon which he had slept, and
he stepped easily onto them with his forefeet, but there
was no room for the rest of him in this box that had
once seemed to him so large.

He stepped away from the carton and explored
through the dimness of the familiar room. Dust was
thick on everything, and three times in succession he
sneezed explosively. On the whole, not much had
changed in here; the rusted metal plant stand near the
door, and against which the door had bumped when it
opened, was not familiar to him, but it was the only
significant object he did not recognize. In one of its
four metal rings was a flowerpot filled with caked earth
and the wizened remains of what had once been a
geranium.

He sniffed about, in and around the clutter of boxes
and cans and well-rusted tools, and then, between two
boxes, something caught his eye. He walked over to it
and studied it carefully. It was a golf-ball-sized tuft of
dirty red yarn to which was still attached a few inches
of old fishing line coated with dust.

At first hesitantly, but then more boldly, he stretched
out a paw and tapped it. The fuzz bounced lightly away
a few inches. He followed and tapped it again and
then, with a strange cry in his throat, he pounced upon
it and bit it and rolled over with it clownishly, tossing it

into the air and catching it, swatting it away and then chasing it again.

At one point he snatched it up and rolled over with it gripped in front paws and mouth. He rolled into the three-foot-high plant holder which tipped over and fell to the floor with a loud crash, breaking the flower pot in half and causing the dried earth within it to crumble into small clods.

The noise startled him, and instantly he threw off the mantle of playfulness that had enveloped him. He looked at the plant holder through narrowed eyes. It seemed as if he suddenly realized this was no place for him.

He moved to the door and was on the verge of stepping outside when he paused with one foot lifted and looked back into the familiar little room. He stood that way for a long while and then opened his mouth and a long, mournful yowling left him, a sustained cry which began loudly and gradually dwindled away to silence.

Without another look at the dim interior, he trotted briskly out of the yard, through the prairie and then into the deep woods beyond. Not once did he stop and in that curious manner raise his nose to sniff and listen and look for something beyond his ken.

In fact, he never did it again.

ABOUT THE AUTHOR

As a youth, ALLAN ECKERT spent much time rambling about the country on his own, living close to nature and depending for survival in large measure upon his ability to hunt and fish and utilize the gifts of nature. The things he learned and the observations he made then, and since, have come uniquely alive in his writings. Such books as *The Great Auk, The Silent Sky* and *Wild Season* have gained him a wide and respectful audience. He is also author of *The Frontiersmen,* the historic re-creation of how the white men wrested the Northwest Territory from its Indian inhabitants. *THE CROSSBREED* is soon to be filmed by Don Meier Productions.

▶ **More Exciting Pathfinders for Your Reading Pleasure!**

☐ FOUR DAYS IN JULY, Cornell Lengyel. The true-to-life story of the men who wrote the Declaration of Independence in 1776. (Abr.) (SP4244—75¢)

☐ THE ADVENTURES OF NEGRO COWBOYS, Philip Durham & Everett Jones. Exciting true stories of Negro cowboys in the old West. Illustrated. (SP4450—75¢)

☐ ROBERT FROST: THE POET & HIS POETRY, David Sohn & Richard Tyre. Includes a photo-filled biography and all of his major poems. (SP4368—75¢)

☐ SPORTS SHORTS, Mac Davis. Amazing illustrated stories about unbelievable but true happenings from the world of sports. (HP4396—60¢)

☐ THE CHAMPION BREED, Al Stump. Action-filled stories of bitter defeats and startling victories of America's great athletes. (HP4256—60¢)

☐ HIROSHIMA. John Hersey's superb story of what happened the day the atom bomb was dropped. (HP4442—60¢)

☐ STOP, LOOK & WRITE!, David Sohn & Hart Leavitt. The creative new way of writing effectively through pictures. (SP4828—75¢)

☐ CHEAPER BY THE DOZEN, Frank Gilbreth & Ernestine Carey. The hilarious story of the twelve lively Gilbreth children. (HP4675—60¢)

☐ THE MIRACLE WORKER, William Gibson. The beautiful, terrifying and inspiring drama of the young helpless Helen Keller. (HP4681—60¢)

☐ LOVE AND SEX IN PLAIN LANGUAGE, Eric Johnson. Everything a young person needs to know is explained with sympathetic understanding. (SP5242—75¢)

☐ THE BRIDGE AT ANDAU, James Michener. The dramatic account of the Hungarian revolt against Communist tyranny. (SP5245—75¢)

☐ UP FROM SLAVERY, Booker T. Washington. The autobiography of the Negro who became a world-famous educator and statesman. (HP4151—60¢)

☐ THE DICTATORS, Jules Archer. Illustrated life stories of the most powerful dictators the world has ever known. (SP4184—75¢)

☐ DAY OF INFAMY, Walter Lord. The vivid recreation of the Japanese sneak attack on Pearl Harbor in 1941. (SP5632—75¢)

☐ A NIGHT TO REMEMBER, Walter Lord. The minute-by-minute account of the sinking of the fabulous ship Titanic. (HP4648—60¢)

☐ THE MAN WHO NEVER WAS, Ewen Montagu. The breathtaking story of the most brilliant and daring spy plot of World War II. (HP4496—60¢)

☐ AFRICA YESTERDAY AND TODAY, Clark Moore & Ann Dunbar, eds. A distinguished collection of essays on Africa's problems and prospects. (HP4156—95¢)

☐ SINK THE BISMARCK!, C. S. Forester. The true story of Hitler's mightiest battleship and how it was hunted and destroyed. (HP5428—60¢)

☐ INHERIT THE WIND, Jerome Lawrence & Robert Lee. The explosive drama, based on a real trial, about teaching evolution in the schools. (HP4324—60¢)

Ask for them at your local bookseller or use this handy coupon:

BANTAM BOOKS, INC., Dept. PNF, Room 2450, 666 Fifth Ave., New York, N. Y. 10019

Please send me the Bantam Pathfinder Editions which I have checked. I am enclosing $_____ (check or money order—no currency please.) Sorry, no C.O.D.'s. Note: Please include 10¢ per book for postage and handling on orders of less than 5 books.

Name_____

Address_____

City_____ State_____ Zip Code_____

Please allow about four weeks for delivery.   PNF—4/70